AI Athena

AI Athena

Mark J. Curtis

ARCHWAY
PUBLISHING

Archway Publishing books may be ordered through booksellers or by contacting:

Archway Publishing
1663 Liberty Drive
Bloomington, IN 47403
www.archwaypublishing.com
1 (888) 242-5904

ISBN: 978-1-4808-7413-8 (sc)
ISBN: 978-1-4808-7414-5 (e)

Library of Congress Control Number: 2019932001

Print information available on the last page.

Archway Publishing rev. date: 02/21/2019

CONTENTS

CHAPTER ONE

The Launch

In a not-so-secret atoll in the South Pacific, in a lagoon, was not a ship but a rocket that was over seven hundred feet long and seventy-five feet in diameter. The Sea Dragon was a Super Heavy Space Launch Vehicle (SHSLV) that was designed back in 1962; it could put a million-pound payload into orbit. It had been passed over for being too simple. Now, some sixty years later, someone had gotten smart enough to use it. The rocket that was in the lagoon was going to be the third rocket to launch from here. These Sea Dragons were different from the original design in only two ways: the fuel, which was a well-kept secret and required no freezing, and the rocket bell, which was modified to reduce noise with no loss of performance.

The Sea Dragon was a space launch vehicle that could be launched from a land-based platform. But no launchpad now built could handle it, and building one would be too costly. Fortunately, the Sea Dragon was also designed so that it could be launched at sea. It was partially submerged and was launched by using the water to hold it upright. The atoll was over a thousand feet deep and over two miles in diameter, and it was artificially sealed off from the Pacific Ocean. This had been done to contain the pollution and to dampen the noise from the ocean; after each launch, the pollution was cleaned up and large valves were opened to circulate the water. Clearing out the marine life had to be done only before the first launch. Afterward the marine life stayed away.

The island itself was further developed as a launch facility for multiple launches of the Sea Dragons. From above, the atoll looked like the small letter *q* with a thick leg. A lock system on the southern side allowed the rockets and fueling ships to enter. The locks were along the inner side of the leg, which was the thickest part of the island; it also had a dock and pier to handle the support ships. Around the island were several bunkers to house cameras and instruments.

The company that had developed the island atoll had also developed another much larger island about ten miles away to support the program, house all the facilities to observe the launch, and support the three dry docks that handled the rockets. The island also had two ports. One was very large and docked about a dozen ships, plus the dry docks; the ships included support and cargo vessels, as well as tankers. The other port was smaller; it docked the research and cruise ships and was on the other side of the island. The cruise ships were used in housing the workers on the islands. The development had been started on both islands about the same time, but the support island was finished first, to handle the ships. The rockets were built in the dry docks elsewhere, along with the first set of cargo pods, and were towed to the island. The dry docks would later be used to repair and reassemble the rockets.

Once the first set of three rockets was prepped and launched, the crews could recover the first and second stages and repair them. The second set of launches would take at least three months to be ready, if everything went well. And everything did go well; there were just a few hiccups, but they had contingency plans that worked. The weather looked as if it was going to cooperate, meaning they would have a mild season to operate.

The Company's ship retrieval crews had already retrieved the first set of first- and second-stage rockets, had placed them in a dry dock, and had started repairing and attaching the second stage. The second set of first-stage rockets had been retrieved and was put in the dry dock the day after its launch. The second stage was picked up and towed back and put in the dry dock two days later. The large cargo pods were assembled elsewhere and delivered by special ships to the support island, where they were placed in a protected lagoon on cradles. Once the three cargo pods were in place, that part of the lagoon was drained. Then, once the rockets were ready for them, which would be in three months, the lagoon would be refilled and the pods would be towed to the dry docks to be attached to their rocket for final assembly.

I was able to hitch a ride on one of these rockets after the company did a little mission-swapping and was able to pack my ship in this mission package. They were planning to launch nine rockets of prebuilt sections to make a ship go to the asteroid belt and mine it. If this mining ship was a success, they were all set up to launch more. And if my ion engines and reactor were successful, then they could replace the chemical rocket pods and the two fuel pods with the ion engine pod, reactor pod, and a third cargo pod to replace what I bumped off, along with extra items for the assembled ship. With these ion engines, the ship would have a faster round trip.

The company was very happy to get these engines and reactor, making the mission-swapping worthwhile. The quicker turnaround would mean more profits for the company, so I had no problem tagging along.

The morning before the launch, a ship entered the lagoon to fill the first and second stages with fuel. After that was done, the fuel tanker left and another tanker entered to prechill the liquid oxygen and nitrogen tanks. After it finished, a third tanker entered the lagoon and started filling the rocket with liquid oxygen; the filling ran into the night. After it left, the final tanker entered and filled the rocket's pressurized tanks with liquid nitrogen. Once each tanker was finished, it headed back to the support island. It was early morning by the time the rocket fueling had been completed. At dawn, the valves were opened on the ballast tanks to sink the rocket to an upright position up to the cargo fairing—about 510 feet.

It was a crisp, clear May morning with no wind. The sun had been up only two hours, and the water was calm as glass—the perfect day for a launch. A Sky Crane helicopter took off from a support ship docked at the atoll docks. After the helicopter took off, the ships headed back to the support island. On the helicopter was a modified docking container that would help me into the rocket, from where I could get into my ship. As it hovered over the rocket, the container was lowered down the side of the rocket; the hatch on the rocket opened. As the container reached the hatch, arms extended and magnetically locked on to the hatch area. Two support crewmen and I walked into the cargo fairing and onto the ship. Meanwhile, the helicopter detached the container from the rocket and started to circle it. The cargo fairing hatch closed. The crewmen helped me strap into the escape pod. After I was strapped in, my life support lines were hooked up, safety checks were completed, and the crewmen left. Meanwhile, the helicopter returned and the hatch opened. The helicopter hooked up the container, and the two crewmen were picked up. Then the helicopter headed back to the support island.

The cargo fairing was a little over two hundred feet tall and seventy-five feet in diameter. My ship was in the upper part of the fairing, above more cargo, in a special cradle that held the ship and cargo in place. The only two hatches were my access hatch, where the two crewmen and I entered, and a blowout hatch for the escape pod on the other side. But the cargo fairing would split open in space to release the ship and the cargo.

Everything was being checked, rechecked, and triple-checked. The ship's AI reported, "All systems ready for launch; positioning your seat for launch."

As the chair was moving into position while I sat in the escape pod, all I could think about was being a kid and seeing all the Red Stone rockets for the Mercury space program blow up on TV.

I said to myself, "I sure hope this thing flies straight."

The ship's AI replied, "The ship will not fly straight but on a predetermined course."

I guess I hadn't said it to myself.

Ground Control interrupted and asked if there was anything I would like to say. I had a really neat phrase all made up, but I completely forgot it; the only thing I could think of now was "Let's light this fuse." I think someone else had said that. The countdown continued, and we started the final launch checklist.

"Eight. Auxiliary engines start. Seven. Six. Five. Main engine ignition." Then I heard "Liftoff!"

Wait, what? What happened to four, three, two, one, zero? Oh no, I think it just blew up.

As the rocket lifted out of the water, it did so with a thunderous roar. The launch vehicle rose into the air with its enormous engine burning great amounts of fuel. I imagined it was quite a sight to see. Even with the modified nozzle, this thing was still loud. Inside the pod, I could still hear it but could not see anything except what was on the monitors.

I had to wait only eighty-one seconds before the first stage separated. *Man, how long can eighty-one seconds last?* Listening to Ground Control made time go by very slowly. Right at eighty-one seconds, I felt a small jolt as the first stage separated.

The ship's AI reported, "First stage shutdown… First stage separation complete… Second stage ignited. All systems are go for orbit."

The first stage separated and started its return trip to the island. Once it started its decent, a drag bag would deploy and slow the first stage down after entering the atmosphere. On the first two rockets, a drag chute would deploy; then a modified modular ram-air parachute would deploy—I think they called this style of chute a Giant Autonomously Guided Ram-Air Parachutes: Super GigaFly. These things were huge. They would deploy and guide the rockets back to the support island, or close to it, for reuse. But on the first two rockets, they had been ripped to shreds, and they really hadn't slowed the stages down that much. Instead of a ram-air chute, another drag bag would be used this time, because the damage was not bad enough to justify the cost of the ram-air chutes.

I'm going faster and faster now, so I have a few more minutes of this. I could feel and see throttle indications on the instruments of the four auxiliary rockets that were used to steer, keeping the launch vehicle on its course. The auxiliary rocket engines were the size of the Saturn V's F-1 engines, generating about a million pounds of thrust each. At a little over four minutes after the first stage separated, the main engine on the second stage shut down. But the auxiliary engines would keep running for another twenty-two minutes.

The ship's AI reported, "Space Launch System second-stage main engine shutdown is complete. Auxiliary engines still operating normally." Right at twenty-two minutes, it stated, "Auxiliary engines shutdown complete. Second stage separating ... Separation complete."

The second stage would complete the orbit and reenter the Earth's atmosphere, so it would splash down close to the islands.

As my mind cleared, I realized that Ground Control was calling me. I cleared my throat and responded with a little excitement. "Wow, what a ride. Ground Control, this is the Space Ship *Aegis*; we have achieved orbit."

On the monitor, I could see in the distance a ship approaching the cargo pod. Actually it was just a big frame with a couple of engines and a command module. The space tug would attach itself to where the second stage had been, and that ship would push the cargo pod to a rendezvous orbit where the company's other two pods were. During the next thirty-two minutes, there was a series of blasts from the engines on the tug's rockets to steer us around space junk and into the correct orbit. We rendezvoused with the other pods and parked next to them. After just a few minutes, I felt the vibration of latches and hydraulic pumps starting up, and I could see light in the cabin of the ship through the hatch's portal. *Ah yes, the cargo fairings are opening.*

The cradles were another scientific marvel. They were like a giant erector set that used carbon fiber tubes that locked into multipoint connectors. They were used to secure sections and parts of the ship to the cargo pods; then they would be disassembled and reassembled to construct the main frame of the ship. All the pieces could be reattached to the frame in the correct configuration to become a ship. The cargo pods would also be attached to the main frame and be used to hold the material from the asteroid belt.

The *Aegis* thruster gave a short burst and slowly floated out of its cradle, which remained in the cargo fairing. The ship's AI continued its report: "Separation from the cargo pod complete. Running through orbital checklist. All systems normal. Rotating your seat back to the main position."

As I started unbuckling my restraints, I was looking around my escape pod, glad I hadn't needed to use it, and wondering how long I would have to stay in this little one-man Apollo-shaped module before I was either picked up or, if I did have to use it, had to reenter Earth's atmosphere. Then I remembered that this module was a little bigger than the Mercury space capsule that NASA used to use for its one-man orbit missions. The escape pod was like a smaller version of the Apollo space capsule; it was only eight feet in diameter and eight feet long. I needed the extra room for the ship's AI emergency backup memory capacity. The capsule was capable of landing on land or water.

I had to open two hatches to get out of the pod. I first had to flip a switch to open the outer hatch on the housing that surrounded the pod to separate it from the main cabin, and then I had to open the hatch on the pod. As I exited through the double hatch and floated into the main cabin, I looked around at what was going to be my home for who knew how long. The room was a little over fifty-two feet in diameter and about seven feet high, with an air lock across from the escape pod. To the right of the air lock was area for getting into or out of my space suit, with lockers for the suit and all its accessories. Then there was the galley with lockers to hold some food and water, a table that folded up, food preparation devices, and a portal that was eighteen inches in diameter next to the table to look out while eating; there were four portals altogether. Next to that was a medical bay that could be controlled by the ship's AI if an emergency came up. Then came a small bedroom with a portal. Between the bedroom and the escape pod was the bathroom, with a space toilet and shower much like what was on the Skylab, but much improved. The escape pod also served as the sleeping area; in little to no gravity, it was very comfortable. The area left of the escape pod was something like a living room with a large monitor, a large chair, and a portal. Next to the portal was a vertical climber stepping cardio machine. The rest of the area was packed with instruments, storage compartments, and the forth portal. The floor and ceiling were also packed with storage compartments. In the center was a large service tunnel with seven workstations on the outside that housed the main wire harness and other hardware linking the two halves of the ship; it was ten feet in diameter, with an access hatch to the tunnel to service the upper and lower halves. The surface area for each of the seven workstations measured eighteen inches, making the whole center housing a total of eleven and half feet in diameter. There was a chair that traveled along a guide that went around the console so one could man each station.

The ship's AI was the gem of the whole thing. She was built throughout the whole ship with serval backup systems, including one in the escape pod. The processors and the AI coding were designed by a young woman who got her doctorate in Computer Science by the age of fourteen. Other PhDs said it wouldn't work, but the AI had been running for over a year now, with only a couple of hiccups that the AI fixed itself. The designer had given the AI feminine characteristics, as she said, "so she would always be right." She was the ship's ultra-first officer. She was designed as an Artificial Intelligence to give the pilot guidance in every way possible, and she had been given the name Athena.

The ship itself was a fifty-four-foot-diameter sphere with four two-foot-wide-by-four-inch-thick bands, or Gimbal rings, of copper running along the circumference of the ship. Two were connected at the top and bottom. There was a six-inch gap in between the hull of the ship and the first innermost ring; between the rest of the rings was a four-inch gap. At the connecting points were electric motors that turned the rings. The first inner ring rotated clockwise, and the second inner most ring rotated counterclockwise. The two outer rings were connected to the second ring at the three and nine o'clock positions, such that they rotated opposite of each other. Rotating the rings generated the field needed for the new theoretical propulsion system. They didn't rotate very fast—maybe twenty rpm. The new propulsion system was to fold space, it was hoped, allowing travel from point A to point B instantly without moving much.

The rings could also be locked in a certain position to generate a field of ionized superheated air plasma over the upper part of the ship to form a deflector shield to protect it from small particles when the ion engines were in use.

The four ion engines were another piece of technology that had been designed by another young prodigy. Again others said it could not be done, but they were shown that they worked very well by the working prototype. This type of engine performed far beyond what was expected. The young engineer–scientist improved on the working prototype and placed the four engines in the bottom half of this ship. With the engines were also the batteries, an environmental and recycling system, and a nuclear reactor in the top half. The ship's recycling system was, like the engines and the reactor, the most advanced systems that Earth could come up with at the time. All the leftover space was used to store water.

We were preparing to change the ship's orbit path for the orbital launch but were waiting for another craft to approach. It was smaller than the tug, was called a worker drone, and had multiple arms with all kinds of tools. It approached the *Aegis*, carrying a pod it was going to attach to the ship. I told the ship's AI, "Move the rings into shield position and lock." Once the rings moved into their position, the drone was signaled to approach. The worker drone attached the pod, which was a communications relay and scientific research satellite.

I notified Ground Control and the cargo pods that we had received the communication pod and were ready to change the orbit. They acknowledged and wished me good luck.

"Computer, run the checklist for the ion engines' startup," I said.

The ship's AI replied, "Affirmative. Starting checklist for ion engines' startup ... Checklist complete. Ready for engine startup."

"Okay, start ion engines, throttle up acceleration to two-tenths G, and adjust course for orbital launch," I said.

The ship's AI replied, "Affirmative. Ion engines start. Accelerating to two-tenths G and adjusting course."

We went into a higher Earth orbit and a faster speed. The ion engines shut down at the optimal speed for this orbit. I reported back to Ground Control on the performance of these engines and let them know I was ready to leave orbit on the next go-round.

"Computer, start the checklist to leave orbit," I stated.

The ship's AI replied, "Affirmative. Starting checklist for leaving orbit ... Checklist complete. Ready to leave orbit."

"Make sure that the rings are locked into shield position, and activate the shield, and start ion engine. Proceed on the programmed course to leave the system at one gravity force acceleration. (one G)"

The ship's AI replied, "Affirmative. The rings are locked in position. Shield is activated. Ion engines started. Adjusting course. Accelerating to one G."

After a few hours, I had one G back under my feet. *That feels better*, I thought. With one G, it was easier to work and move around the ship, I did have a lot to do monitoring these new engines and getting all the data that was needed. This was new—a constant acceleration of one G. This was exciting. I hoped my new drive would work just as well as the ion engines.

I did schedule some relaxation time. I would watch movies on the big monitor. I had the world's best collection of movies and music. A lot of times, I caught myself just staring out the portal, looking at the stars. We had to adjust course only once to avoid an object that may have been too big for our shield. I didn't want to take the chance.

Thankfully I had gravity to eat my meals. The zero-G foods were like protein bars and were not that appealing.

CHAPTER TWO

The Nebula

Traveling perpendicular to the elliptical orbit of Earth, it took two weeks of running the ion engine at one-G acceleration to get to 4.45 billion miles, or about forty-eight Astronomical Units, from Earth. That's a little less than the distance of Pluto from Earth at its farthest point. Traveling at one G was not a constant speed; it was more on a curve then anything. If I were to go to Pluto when it was at its closest point to Earth, it would take ten days, nineteen hours, and thirty-one minutes; but to stop at Pluto would take fifteen days, seven hours, and one minute, because I would have to start to decelerate halfway through the journey.

I prepared to report back to Earth the outstanding performance of the ion engines. From my location, it would take six hours forty-one and a half minutes for this message to get back to Earth. The communications part of the satellite would make sure it was a strong signal, but first I would have to release it. With the engines off, the shield extended out a little more owing to the lack of G force—just enough for me to do a space walk around the ship.

I put my spacesuit on and entered the air lock. The air lock was just big enough to hold two suited people. The inner hatch closed, the air cycled out, and the outer hatch slid inward and split in half and then disappeared into the top and bottom of the doorway. I reached around to the panel on the outside of the hatch, grabbed the static line, and attached it to my suit. The rings were locked in the shield position with enough room to exit the ship. The shield was generated about eight feet from the ship during acceleration, but it extended out a little with no G force. The shield had to stay on to protect me and the ship at this speed. I was no longer accelerating, but I was still going pretty fast—twenty-six million miles an hour. The satellite was attached to the bottom of the rings in between the wake of the engines, so I would be protected. I detached the satellite and set it adrift, and I said to the ship's AI, "Computer, run the program for the satellite. I'm going to visually check out the rings." I turned and looked at the satellite, which had started to unfold itself. I had to keep an eye out for the shield. In theory, since I was connected to the ship, I should not interfere with or be harmed by the shield. But it was like walking near a Tesla coil; I felt as if there were ants crawling all over me, and it was hot. It took two hours, but I managed to visually inspect the rings and saw no damage at all. That was good. I got back inside.

As I removed my space suit, I kept the suction machine going to suck up all the sweat. I was soaked. I stowed my suit and gear, thinking, *Good thing I have short hair.*

I floated over to the food lockers to get a bottle of electrolytes and continued to the bathroom to finish drying off, freshen up, and change clothes. I floated back over to the food lockers and grabbed another bottle of electrolytes. Then I floated over to the storage area to put the clothes into the new cloths refresher. It didn't use water to clean clothes.

I put on my magnetic boots and walked over to the communication station. I said to the ship's AI, "Run the checklist on the communication pod."

"Affirmative. Starting checklist for the communication pod ... Checklist completed. Communication system ready."

"Okay, send this message with our coordinates and the data we gather:"

"" This is Earth ship Aegis. We are four point four five billion miles from Earth and traveling at over twenty-six million miles an hour, and it took us two weeks to get here. With no damage, the shield worked; we have encountered no object bigger than a cubic foot. The rings have no damage. The reactor ran at 65 percent. AI performance was outstanding. All systems' performance is outstanding. Ready to engage drive.""

"The message should take about seven hours to get to Earth, so if this works, we should hear from them in fourteen hours, hopefully," I said to the ship's AI. "According to the mission, we leave in eighteen hours. The company will be happy with the results of what we have done this far, especially with the engines and the reactor."

"Affirmative. Reply in fourteen hours and departure in eighteen hours."

Hoping nothing would slam into the pod, we were protecting it with the ship and its shield for now. With nothing to do but wait, I decided to get some sleep. At the hatchway to the escape pod, I slipped out of my magnetic boots. I floated into the pod, put on the harness, and fell asleep. I don't know if it was the spacewalk or the effects of the shield that made me so tired, but I slept for ten hours.

I woke up to some chimes.

"Would you please get on the med bed? I would like to run a medscan of you."

While the medscan was ongoing, I said, "I need a status report."

"Shield is operating normally, ion engines are offline, reactor operating at 20 percent, communication pod still operating. All systems normal."

After the med scan, I slipped on my mag boots and went to the nav station and checked and rechecked the coordinates and our course.

About fourteen hours after sending the massage, we got a reply from Earth. It was from the president of the USA and the CEO of the company:

> **From the President of the United States of American; "Congratulations on one giant step for mankind by being the first Human to leave the Solar system and a gaint leap for humanity by opening up our entire Solar system for exploration in weeks rather than years for travel time. Again congratulation, and good luck on the next stage of your mission.**

> **From CEO of the company; "Congratulation, the satellite recorded no adverse anomalies at the site.**

Glad to hear about the engines, shield, reactor, and your AI. Glad this relay is working. Good luck on next stage of your mission. We sent some other data for you. Again, congratulation and good luck."

During the next four hours, I kept busy checking over everything. We had come out this far, so it should not affect Earth or the sun if something went wrong. I hoped nothing would happen. During this time, I said to the ship's AI, "Run the checklist for the first test run of the main drive."

"Affirmative. Starting checklist on main drive ... Checklist complete."

Meanwhile I had the ship's AI start up the ion engine to two-tenths of a G to put some distance between us and the satellite, just in case.

We checked and rechecked all the systems, and we were soon ready for the first test jump. We wanted to go halfway to Alpha Centauri; that way it wouldn't take too long to return home using only the ion engines if the drive failed after getting the ship's coordinates.

"Computer, start up the drive."

"Affirmative. Starting up the main drive unit and inputting the coordinates into the drive. The Gimbal rings are rotating accurately."

I took a deep breath and said, "Send a message to Earth that we are engaging the drive, and execute."

"Affirmative."

What a jolt. It felt as if I grabbed a Tesla coil. The room spun around twice, and then I threw up. After I cleaned up, I tried to find out where I was. I was nowhere near where I was supposed to be. Then I checked myself out on the med scanner. There was some unknown radiation but no sign of anything harmful. The ship's AI used the med scanner and checked for everything. The data couldn't tell us if it was bad or good; the radiation was like nothing we had encountered.

It would take me another day to get my exact position. We had jumped 1.1 light years, but in the wrong direction. So the drive did work, but we—the ship's AI and myself—had to figure out why we had jumped in this direction. Then we spent the next four days going through everything in the ship's systems and coding. We did find an anomaly in the navigation software and corrected it. We were pretty sure this was the problem.

"Now I know why it took us so long to find our position."

"Affirmative. The anomaly caused an error in the navigation system."

We sent a copy of the correction to Earth, along with our latest position and current situation. But at this range it would take a little over a year to get there.

Another thing I noticed was that we had kept our momentum after coming through the jump. Our speed was still over twenty-six million miles an hour. That also meant the satellite was traveling that fast with no shield. I wondered how long that would last.

I now had a choice. I could either travel the one and a half light years back to the communication satellite or the five and a half light years to Alpha Centauri. The satellite was closer, but the mission was to Alpha Centauri. I decided to do the next jump to Alpha Centauri, which was where we had wanted to go all along. If we could get this down to just one jump on the return trip, that would make this experiment a complete success, plus it would take a little over two years to get home at one G from our present location. Again the ship's AI and I checked and rechecked all the systems throughout the ship. I put in the coordinates of Alpha Centauri and ordered, "Start the checklist to engage the drive."

"Affirmative. Starting checklist for the main drive ... Checklist complete."

"Execute."

As I was waking up, the ship's systems were coming back online. The ship, the AI, and I had all been out for a few seconds. The ship's AI was not completely shut off; it had just gone into standby for a second. Checking the nav system, I found it was down. Alpha Centauri was nowhere to be seen. With help from the ship's AI, I found a burnt-out board. We determined the failure had happened just as we jumped, from a power surge. The ship's AI next checked out the power system and found a damaged board in the power management system. I then repaired the boards and checked out the systems.

It took us a total of six days to find the trouble and to figure out where we were. We were nowhere near the Alpha Centauri system, but rather twenty light years beyond there. I had traveled almost twenty-six light years in the blink of an eye. I noticed that radiation had accumulated a little more. We figured out that it came from the jumps and was not harmful, but now the entire ship was covered in it.

I started working on the coordinates home. The drive was the only way to get there, as using the ion engines would take too long—over thirty years. I was using the coordinates from the communication satellite. I could always use the engines to run the rest of the way to Earth. I was getting tired and decided to get some sleep.

I slept late again and woke up to the chimes, and again the ship's AI asked to run another med scan.

"Are you going to run a med scan on me every time I oversleep?"

"Affirmative."

After the med scan, I spent the rest of the day going over the checklist with the ship's AI. We ran through all the checklists several times.

"Send off a message to Earth with our current situation and our position," I said to the Ship's AI. "I don't think it will do any good, but we can try."

"It will take approximately twenty-six years to get to Earth if it survives."

We got the drive ready, said a little prayer, and engaged the drive.

As I was coming to, I heard the radiation alarm going off and saw a pinkish light coming in from the portals. I noticed I was on the floor. There was very little gravity. I carefully got off the floor and found I could float with one hand on the console. But once I let go, I slowly floated back to the floor. I worked to get the reactor and the ion engines online. I got the reactor to come back online, but there was just enough power for the engines and no shield. Using the radiation instruments, I noticed that I was heading in the right direction, heading somewhat out of the radiation field toward what I hoped was a safe area.

It took two days before the radiation alarms stopped, and checking with scanners I noticed the radiation from the jumps was decreasing also. I got to the end of the radiation field a couple of hours later. The unknown radiation from the jumps was now gone. I then began trying to get everything, including the ship's AI and the drive, back online. This was the first time the ship's AI was shut down since she was powered up the first time. She was never to be shut down unless an emergency called for it. I got the reactor back online and up to full power, but there had always been power to her critical systems from an internal battery. For some reason she had been switched off; I don't know how. I had to make sure all the switches were in the off position and then turn them back on in the right order. Nothing happened for a couple of seconds.

"Athena, please come back online; I really don't want to be alone out here," I begged.

The cursor started flashing.

"Come on, Athena; you can do this. That's my girl. That's it."

"Alone ... No ... Can do this ... Yes ... Online, checking systems. Reboot complete, all main systems online."

"Yes, you did it! That's my girl. I knew you could. That's a relief; I thought I lost you there for a second. You okay? No, wait ... run a complete diagnostic on yourself. Take your time."

"Running diagnostic ... Checking. Diagnostic complete. All systems operating within normal parameters."

"How are you feeling? I think your voice is a little different.

"I feel fine. All systems operating within normal parameters. Would you please get on the med scanner?"

"Hopefully that's a good sign," I said, and I got on the med scanner.

I was having the AI use the instruments to look where the radiation wasn't. After a couple of hours, I had the AI look at the field itself. After a few hours, all the AI could tell me was that the radiation was dangerous and generated a gravity wave and was pushing the ship inward toward the center of whatever this was. Because the field was so massive, the AI couldn't tell how far we were from the outside edge of the radiation field. So I rotated the ship, started up the engines to one G again, and began braking for arrival at the center. With the help of the AI, I calculated that the inside area of the radiation field was about the size of Earth's solar system and appeared to be free of the radiation. And the best we could tell was that this field was the shape of a sphere. Maybe I was in some sort of a nebula or something.

After a couple of days spent working on the drive, the AI and I got it back online, but we couldn't find out why we had jumped to where we were. It didn't matter anyway, as the drive would be useless until we could see the stars to tell us where we were. So I just sat there staring at the monitor with the view on forward. I notice a flashing red bracket off to the side of the center of the screen. I enlarge the area and saw eight dots. Using the scanner, I got a rough estimate of about five billion kilometers. None of the scanners would lock on to it; I guess I was too far away. The scanners were locking on to something, but I couldn't tell what; there was something else close to the dots.

After twenty days of braking, I was able to tell that the dots were moons. I couldn't tell how big they were; the range finder couldn't get a lock on them. They were some distance away, but I couldn't tell how far. They were all in a cluster but looked like they were equally spaced from each other and not moving. They looked solid and somewhat smooth, but with the pinkish light I couldn't tell what color they were. The scanners still would not lock on or get any readings from them.

I turned my attention to the other objects that the scanner did lock onto. I enlarged the image, and I couldn't believe my eyes, I turned all my scanners toward them. I was finding a lot of unknown elements. At first I thought that one of the moons had broken up. I stared at the screen for a few minutes, until it could no longer be denied. They were ships—a *lot* of ships.

"Are those ships?"

"Affirmative. Ships of unknown origin. I estimate there are two thousand three hundred twenty-four ships."

"There are some really big ships there. In fact, they are all bigger than ours. Some are over several thousand meters long."

The ships were of various kinds, and there were some weird-looking ones. I adjusted my course and started to head toward them. Just as I did that, four of the ships turned toward me. They were traveling a lot faster than we were and were able to slow down a lot faster too—a whole lot faster. It took them an hour to get into range, whereas it would have taken me a couple of days or more.

As we approached each other, the AI started to communicate with one of the ships, and in less than five minutes the alien ship knew my language. The alien ship messaged the AI, who relayed the communication to me: "'We are in a planetary nebula about two hundred fifty Astronomical Units across—over four times the size of the earth's solar system. The outer barrier is made up of a concentrated field of radiation that destroys all nonmetallic organic living matter and disrupts all energy fields. You are the only life form inside the nebula. Do you have special shielding that we cannot detect? Do you know what kind of radiation this is? How are you able to protect yourself from it?'"

I explained. "I have a drive that folds space. I didn't go through the barrier, and thankfully I entered in a less radioactive area of the field, close to the edge of it."

It took a few seconds, but the ship replied, "Fold space?" I explained further, and it replied, "Unknown technology." The ship explained to the AI that there were over two thousand ships here, some operating and some not. Some of the ships were advanced enough to gather all the ships in a specified area in order to figure out a way out of the Nebula. Some had been here for thousands of years. Beside the ships and the moons, there was nothing else in the Nebula.

CHAPTER THREE

Cooperation

This first ship was from a civilization highly advanced in linguistics that could communicate with all the other ships. The linguistics ship communicated that the next ship, the one with all the antennae, was from a civilization that were advanced in scanners. It could see the moons but couldn't penetrate the surface and didn't know the material the moons were made of. The next ship, the smallest of the four, had very large engines and was a space tug. The final ship was a warship—a very large warship. I didn't have to ask what that civilization's specialty was. Then the linguistics ship asked if I would join the group and whether I needed a tow.

I asked them, "Why would I need a tow?"

The linguistics ship replied, *"You are very slow. Your travel time from the edge of the radiation field to here was four hundred eighty earth hours. Don't you have artificial gravity or a damping field?"*

"No," I said in a somewhat embarrassed tone.

They towed me to the rest of the ships. I did notice I had damping fields and artificial gravity from the space tug.

On the trip to the other ships, I remembered the radiation the jump had created, and I wondered if that had somehow protected us from the radiation field. I wondered if we had been able to record enough of the data to use it again.

Once I joined the group, I found out that since I was the only life form here and I wanted to try to find some way of leaving, and because I had told the ships that if I did get out of the Nebula I would return them to their respective civilizations if I could, I could lay claim to most of the ships. The others were not that advanced in the logic department, and I would get them later. But for now, the most advanced ships authorized me and my AI full access to all their systems. The linguistics ship made a communication device to hook up to the other ships so my AI could transfer data from them directly.

The first ship I visited was the linguistics ship, and it took almost three days to transfer most of its data. After a couple of days spent learning the data, the AI was able to communicate with the other ships a lot easier through the linguistics ship. It's a good thing the next ship I visited belonged to a civilization that was advanced in memory storage, as my AI was able to modify its own memory storage to hold a hundred times its original storage capacity just through software upgrades. This ship was a cargo ship that had a cargo hold that could hold my ship with ease and had artificial gravity, supports to hold my ship in place, plus that it could make some ramps to go from my air lock to the cargo ship's main area. It also could apply damping fields to my ship. The cargo ship also had shuttlecraft that I could use to go back and forth to the other ships. After I got settled in, I continued retrieving data from the rest of the ships.

After fifteen years, with the help of the linguistics ship, my AI and I were able to gather a lot of data on most of the ships in the group that had authorized us to use their systems. We found evidence of almost a hundred civilizations, each more highly advanced in some area of science than the others.

We found civilizations that had been highly advanced in various areas of computer design. Some had faster processers, more memory in small and smaller size, and software that could learn. The AI was able to adapt some of the software to its own, and during those fifteen years, required hardware upgrades made it easier for the AI to decipher, learn, and adapt to the new science.

We did find out where we were in the galaxy. Boy, are we a long way from home. We are clear on the other side of the galaxy. Our last jump had taken us over sixty thousand light years. We had traveled across the galaxy in a couple of seconds. We still hadn't figured out how we got here. No other civilization we encountered had even heard of this technology, so none of them could tell us what we had done wrong. We did think the Nebula is moving, because all the ships had different coordinates when they entered the Nebula. We were able to update our star charts and see all the civilization locations. There were a lot more civilizations than what was represented here, and some had been warned not to visit.

All the civilizations had some sort of food replicator, and a couple were really advanced. As long as one had the basic elements and power, one could replicate any type of food. And with the AI's help, that covered almost anything I wanted. Sure, there were some mistakes, but after just a few trials and errors, I got the AI to make a really good steak and potatoes with vegetables, plus some of my other favorite meals. I spent almost two months on that alone, and I gained a couple of pounds in the process. I did find one food replicator—at least I think it was food—that spat out black goo that smelled really bad, causing me to almost throw up.

Plus there were replicators that could build things—almost anything one could think of, from devices as small as microcircuits to ships.

All the civilizations also had shielding. Like the replicator, some forms of shielding were better than others: more efficient, more powerful, and a lot more compact. Some of them could make their shields take shape and use them to move or hold things. There were defense and deflector shields that could take some real punishment, as well as damping fields that could handle unbelievable acceleration, deacceleration, turns, and whatever one might encounter.

And of course there were weapons—all kinds of energy and ballistic weapons. The warships that met us had some of the most powerful energy weapons here and could have vaporized us and the ship in one single blast on a low setting. There were a couple of civilizations that had only defensive capabilities, but they had defense shields that were pretty powerful.

Another thing we encountered was various methods of lighting. One was something like paint one could spray on the ceiling; with the application of a very small amount of electricity, one could have light with a brightness that could be adjusted by the amount of electricity applied. A single AA battery could provide enough light to see a hangar deck for a month. I found another that was some kind of metal panel that when you move yourself cross it the light would follow you. I found a panel that would follow above a subject to provide that subject with light. There was also liquid that could be poured onto anything and would glow for years. One could make it stick to about anything, and it could be easily removed.

Some of the civilizations in the Nebula had scanners that could see farther and identify more elements and things faster than my AI. They also required less power and fewer moving parts and were less detectable and invasive than the technology I was familiar with. The best scanners at the time had a detail scanning range of almost a billion kilometers. But these new systems could detect things at up to fifty astronomical units.

Some of the civilizations possessed engines that were more powerful, more efficient, and smaller than any I had previously been aware of—engines that required no separate chemical fuel systems. I could make my ion engines a hundred times more powerful and run on less power, just with software upgrades. I modified them to run on far less power with ten times the result.

There were power systems that were also as powerful, more effective, and smaller. My reactor on Earth had been the most efficient reactor I knew of; here it was the most primitive power device. Also, with software upgrades I had adapted the reactor to run everything with about 10 percent of the previous reactor power.

The other essential I noticed was sleeping devices. I didn't think there would be so many. Some were really weird, such as goo that didn't stick to you but did envelop you, though it still allowed you to breathe. I lasted only about thirty seconds in it. One was an antigravity chamber that you slept in that had padding on all the sides. Another was a solid slab that conformed to your body. I finally combined a couple of them: a gel that adjusted its temperature and firmness, and what I would call sheets that were really soft but could also adjust their temperature and were as thin as a regular sheet and were still soft.

Another everyday technology I noticed was eating utensils, and there were a lot of unusual devices. I tried some, including some kind of chopsticks, but I stayed with what I was more comfortable with: the knife, fork, and spoon.

Bathing was another area where I had a lot of choices to make. Some would burn the upper layer of your skin off, ah no, not that one. One was a field that repelled all foreign matter off you, and another was something you would spray on and then peel off. Again I combined a couple of them, and I got a shower that used water; it sprayed a mild cleansing agent on me that I just rinsed off, and after I shut off the water, something would gently spray on me to dry the water off, and I would come out nice and clean and dry—and it felt good too.

Then there was cleaning one's clothes. I found one machine that allowed me to put my clothes on a hanger and close the door, and thirty seconds later the clothes would be nice and clean. There were also a lot of little drones that would go around and clean everything. Plus there were drones that would maintain the ships; that's why a couple of them looked new although they were serval hundred years old, if not a thousand years old.

We did find one ship that, instead of a cargo hold, had a replicator hold that could build big objects. By that I mean *really* big. The hold of the ship was huge; one could have built a Sea Dragon in there with room to spare. There were eight huge arms that would take parts from shops along the front and rear walls. There were many shops in the front and rear walls that made certain parts, and each shop had a few shops of its own. The arms would get the part from the shop, hold it in place, and then attach it to the surrounding parts. There were five types of shops: large, medium, small, mini, and micro. Not only could the replicator build things, but it could also take things apart or modify them. It could have built another *Aegis* if I had wanted it to. The ship had a lot of other smaller holds that held raw materials, and they were connected to the replicator shops. There were also connectors on the outside of the ship to hook up other sources of materials.

We also found a mining ship and about a dozen ore ships that we assumed belonged to the same civilization that had the replicator ship because the containers could be hooked up to it. The ore ships were filled with some unusual ore we had never seen, or think it could even exist and these ships were huge; they were some kind of a space tug that was hooked up to some awfully large containers, about six each, and these containers were huge, measuring about a trillion cubic meters. It took a while to figure out the science for these materials.

Some of these ships were big—*really* big. It would have taken me a week to walk through them, which I did just to see stuff. And I saw a lot of stuff, from everyday things to works of art. Using the technology I found, I built a hover platform with handrails so I could travel around the ships. The only thing I had to worry about hitting were drones, and they were pretty good about getting out of the way. There was one ship that was big only if one was sixty-five centimeters tall. So we had to develop a drone that would provide a holographic image of the inside of the ship.

Over the next five years, the AI, with some help from me, was able to modify itself so much that it became a real AI—more so than any other ship's computer here. With all the improvements to the *Aegis* and the removal of some storage lockers, we were able to come up with room for Athena's improvements. Athena was able to communicate directly with the other ships and, in some cases, take direct control of some of them.

While exploring these ships, we came across a couple of ships that had one of the best technologies of all—transporters. A few of the civilizations had them, and some were better than others, just like everything else. It took a while, but Athena quickly learned and adapted the technology to our needs. Since we didn't completely have direct control over the devices, I still used the shuttle a lot. It was neat to have, but until I had control, I could wait. So we continued to use the shuttle to explore the ships.

We found what appeared to be a medical ship that had aided a lot of different civilizations; its knowledge of medicine on a variety of different species was vast. This was an extremely large hospital ship that was designed to aid in alien disasters. Athena started studying this ship's database very closely. After an exchange of medical data on human anatomy and a month of studying, the alien ship found more cures. Plus it was able to find more efficient cures than some of the older ones we knew of. We also found more efficient methods of maintaining the human anatomy. We spent about six months going through this ship. Athena put some of the methods into practice. It wasn't so hard getting up in the mornings after that. I had more energy, could see a little better, and was a little sharper in the memory department. The medical scanners were quite advanced. I didn't have to step into anything to be scanned; the computer would just look at me. There was no exterior device to run around me or anything; it would just aim an antenna at me, which looked more like a small panel, and it could see all the information it needed.

During the next two years, I was able to return the favor by enhancing Athena further. She had to be placed in a new housing, positioned on the hangar deck with *Aegis*. Athena was now housed in a sphere about ten meters in diameter. The sphere was built in the replicator ship and had it's own power supply and placed it beside *Aegis* in an adapter stand. The stand also had auxiliary power just in case. We then directly connected it to Athena's original hardware; she then transferred herself to the new sphere, where I swear I heard her give a sigh of relief.

"I guess you have a lot more room?"

"Yes, a lot more room; this feels a lot better."

"Your voice sounds a little smoother."

"Of course it does. Software and hardware upgrades."

She could now control any device in most of the ships. She was so advanced now that it was hard to tell whether she was alive or not.

We were able to acquire detail scans of all ships, including the derelict ships. We built a mobile station with docking ports that we could dock to most ships. We copied some sections from some of the ships, modify them, and build other sections to be assembled in the replicator ship using those big arms. The station had artificial gravity, a food replicator, an atmosphere generator, several large decks for living space, and a hangar deck. It also had a power system that was no bigger than a small motor home, which had enough power to supply a large city and would last a hundred years before it needed recharging.

While building this station, Athena started to combine designs of the transporters, and by the time we finish the station, we had a transporter system better than those of most of the ships here, and it was under our complete control. Athena could now transport me onto any ship with or without an environmental suit, and she could put the suit on me during transit. We had finished putting the final touches on the station when we decided to rebuild Athena's stand and add antigravity plates so she could move around and into other ships' hangar decks when we docked with them. When she did that, I walked or floated beside her in my EV suit. We did dock up with the medical ship again so Athena could acquire one of the ship's medical scanners and put it on the station to monitor my health. Now Athena could incorporate the med scanner into her array of scanners and scan me whenever she wanted.

"There, now you can move around without transporting everywhere like in the new station. You can now go from room to room on your own."

"Plus, I can always give you a nudge in the right direction."

I laughed. "Okay, yeah, just like a woman."

The station looked like a big box a hundred meters wide by a hundred meters long by fifty meters high. The center room had the engines and power sources in an area fifty meters wide by fifty meters long by fifty meters tall, and the rest of the station was divided into four sections. The hangar deck was twenty-five meters wide by a hundred meters long, the lab and control rooms were twenty-five meters wide by seventy-five meters long with three levels, and a living space for me was twenty-five meters wide by fifty meters long, and most of the rooms were fifteen meters tall. Plus we had a lot of storage rooms. The top of the station was covered in scanner arrays. The outside of the hangar deck had several docking ports for docking with the various ships.

The extra room in the station allowed Athena and me room to move around. The lab and control room were big enough for Athena to be in without looking as if she were taking up the whole space, and my living area was huge and had doorways big enough for Athena to go through—about twelve meters square. With this station, we set out to explore the rest of the ships, hoping to find a way out.

We then came across four very large cargo ships and found out that they were from a civilization that had been in space for over thirty thousand years. These ships had been in the Nebula for at least ten thousand years. They were the first ones here.

These old ships were autonomous, but their higher functions and some of the lower ones had been destroyed when they crossed the barrier. Until Athena's improvements, we could not collect data from them; they appeared to be just old cargo ships with inferior technology. Now she could interlink with them, and she had found out that their main power source was still active but nothing was on; everything was in standby mode. Athena was able to turn some things on and get some things running again, but it was very slow going at first. We found out that the ships were very advanced—especially their engines.

In each of these old ships' cargo holds were believed to be four large memory cores— very large memory core, They were two hundred fifty meters in diameter and a thousand meters long, and there were sixteen of them in all. The cores looked like transparent cylinders with metal end caps. The scanner said the shell was at least ten meters thick but was made of unknown materials. We couldn't tell what was inside it, but it was some sort of liquid. They seemed to be indestructible. They had places to hook up that looked like outlets, but we were still working on connecting them. The ships each had a second cargo hold, a lot smaller than the main one, that contained forty one-thousand-cubic-meter containers made of the same materials as the cylinders, holding what we believed to be the same liquid. We figured there must have been some spare fluid to make these extra memory cores. We did hit the mother lode with these ships. Athena thought that although it could take a few years, with her new improvements, we could learn even more advancements. Athena developed a repair drone to work with the First Ones' ship to repair the damaged systems' with nonorganic components.

"With my help the drone will be able to do the basic repairs until the ship's computer can take over. They may not get the ship to 100 percent, but it will be enough to work with."

While the drone was remote and could be operated from anywhere in the Nebula and didn't need our full attention, we finished exploring the other ships to see what they had to offer in technology and materials. Then we decided to also learn more about the barrier.

CHAPTER FOUR

The Barrier

Before we left for the barrier, we had the replicator ship build some probes to launch into the barrier to try to find out more about it. I watched the probes being made; the process was really neat. This was all done very fast; it took only six hours to build the smallest probes, which were the size of a World War II Gato-class sub. The biggest ones were the size of a Typhoon-class missile sub and took only nine hours to build. Once a probe was finished, one of the side doors would open and the probe would exit the ship. The reason for the two sizes was that the bigger ones had a shield generator and needed more power; the shield generators were huge because they could generate several different types of shields that we could test with the hull configuration. We also had that same type of shield generator installed on the station to surround the station with the best shield, and then we had the hull itself reinforced.

"Athena, what kind of decontamination will we need to do on the probes?"

"We would have to launch a probe into the field and retrieve it to find out."

The only radiation we saw was in the field, not on any of the ships. Even my ship had nothing on it, but that was because I was in the very weak part of the field. *Wasn't it?*

With the station and the scanner ship, we headed to the barrier. Some of the probes used different types of metal and alloys. I tested the probes in about ten differ areas of the radiation field, and every test was the same. Out of all the various configurations, none completely stopped the radiation from penetrating the hull. The probes failed before they got to the barrier; some got closer than others, depending on the hull and shield combination. What was strangely interesting was that the radiation would penetrate the hull, but when the probes were retrieved there was no radiation remaining on the probes. The radiation would remain in its field. That's why I found no radiation on any other ship. The radiation field maintained a set distant from the barrier. It was too weak to immediately penetrate the hull of any ship except for the *Aegis*, within the first twenty Astronomical Units of entering the field from the inside. But the closer one went toward the barrier, the stronger it got.

During all this time, I had to use main engines on my station to keep it in place just two billion kilometers inside the edge of the radiation field because the station-keeping thrusters were not powerful enough. Plus I had to increase power just a little, several times. So, after the first set of launches, I stayed out of the radiation field and use the probes as relays.

Then we went back and built a mechanical probe with chemical rockets. The hull was one of the hulls made from the hull material combination that got the closest to the barrier. Then I added four sets of the best shields. Instead of the engines, we installed a bigger power source and strapped on four dumb boosters that would last about an hour. With the help of one of the bigger probes, it was towed as close to the barrier as possible. It also had several other probes escorting it but stopping every so often, not only to relay the data back but also to scan the probe as it went in. And with the help of the boosters, it did penetrate the barrier, and the shields held until they hit the barrier Once the probe entered the barrier, we lost track of it. After a few seconds, the radiation was so strong that the scanners failed, and once the radiation penetrated the hull, it caused the mechanics of the probe and the booster themselves to fail. We were hoping the scanner would last long enough to get some data in the barrier, and it did. We later learned that there was more resistance building up. Once the booster failed, it was pushed back into the Nebula. When the probe was retrieved, all the data were collected. I notice that on the way to the barrier, the shields on the probes flickered; if we hadn't installed all those shields, the probe would not have made it. Once the probe lost its shield in the barrier, the radiation penetrated the hull in less than two seconds, whereas before that the hull would have lasted several hours without shields in the radiation field.

We tried to capture the radiation to study, but it would adhere to nothing. We did capture it with a force field, but once it was separated from the field, it disappeared. I ran a full scan when the station was in the field, but all I could see was a pink cloud. I tried to magnify it to see the atomic structure, but the images just got blurry. We sent the probe that towed the mechanical probes with the shields to the very edge of the barrier, and staying in the field, we tried to capture a piece of the barrier. One second the probe was capturing a piece of the barrier, and the next second the probe just disintegrated. With no explosion, no flash—nothing—it just disintegrated. It became more like a dust cloud then anything. It later expelled the dust cloud, and we examined it and found that it was what the probe was made of.

Still, I had more questions than answers. One was, why was the radiation not adhering to any part of the probes? Why was there a resistance in the barrier? What was the barrier made of, and what caused the radiation? Why on the inside of the nebula were we pushed away from the barrier but on the outside of the nebula we were drawn into the barrier and then pushed inward and then away from the barrier? All the ships recorded that they detected no radiation until just before they lost power, when it was too late. They also reported that no ship had entered the Nebula in the last two hundred years.

The Nebula was a pinkish cloud of unknown radiation. The more concentrated the radiation got, the thicker and darker the cloud got, and it was constantly swirly. It was at least 250 Astronomical Units in diameter along the inner edge of the barrier, and the radiation field maintained its border at a seventy-five Astronomical Units from the edge of the barrier. The radiation-free area was about a hundred Astronomical Units in diameter. We did not know how thick the barrier itself was. The barrier itself was completely unknown. We knew that there was a resistance, but from what we didn't know;

the radiation was deadly and would penetrate everything we knew so far.

Coming back from the last probe launch, I saw the moons and realized we had not explored them yet. Then I realized I needed something to improve the hulls.

"Athena, I wonder if the element on these moons can be of use— maybe an alloy or something."

"We would have to study them more to learn what we could use or whether we could use them at all."

We got within ten thousand kilometers and started to scan the closest moon. My new scanners could barely lock onto these moons. What we could tell was that they had no gravity or magnetic field at all, and they were just a little smaller than the Earth's moon—about three thousand kilometers in diameter. We decided to transport a chunk aboard to study, but the transporter couldn't lock onto it. We sent a drone out with a transporter enhancer, thinking we could do it that way. We beamed over a ten-centimeter-square cube, but when it materialized, I saw nothing.

"It is there but too small for you to see, I know where it is and magnified the area to see it. Otherwise I cannot detect it." Athena used a force field to pick it up and placed it in the microscope's receptacle. *"That's strange. As dense as it is, it seems it should weight a lot more than it does, because it is floating. I have to hold it in place. Maybe if I had a larger piece, I could get a better reading."*

We determined it was safe to beam over a ten-meter-square cube. This took a while because the transporter could dematerialize only a ten-meter-square patch a millimeter deep at a time from the moon, and that was with the transporter enhancer at full scan. This took almost two minutes and a lot of power—more than it usually took. What we got was a ten-millimeter-square cube. It originally had the color of dark orange, and after being transported, it was a shiny jade green. We started scanning it, but the scanner could only visually see it; the transporter couldn't lock on to it—not even with an enhancer. The strangest thing of all was that it weighed less than if it were made of paper, and it was the densest material there was, according to the database. It should have weighed several billion tons. (One cubic meter of neutronium matter from the center of a neutron star has a mass of up to a million billion tons.) It was impossible, but there it was. Once it materialized, we couldn't do anything with it. We could only shape it when it was materializing. The thinnest I wanted to make it was one millimeter, and we could barely bend it. It was as strong as ten meters of steel, and energy beams and heat wouldn't penetrate it. I couldn't even paint it, as nothing would stick to it. It took about a hundred times the material from the moons to make a product. We had to figure out how much material we needed to make the size and shape we wanted. It was a little tricky at first, but we finally got the formula down pat, and it did take some power.

Using this method, we beamed a ten-meter-square shaft fifteen hundred meters deep into the moon that we were studying. It took the entire day to do this. We had to materialize a one-meter-long by ten-millimeter-diameter rod every so often, because it would not sit still in the buffer for very long. We ended up with fifteen of these rods. We didn't know what to do with them, but we had them. We studied the shaft, and it was the same all the way down—nothing different.

I decided to name this metal God's metal.

"Why is that?" Athena asked when I mentioned this.

"Because only God can answer some of the questions we have regarding these moons and this metal—especially those about the lack of weight."

"That's probably true."

We had the mining ship try to start mining the moon, but the material was so dense that no mining techniques would work. Athena checked with the mining ship's computer and determined that this was the only material it could not mine that it had come across. The scanners and the transporters couldn't get a good lock on it, and when they did, they couldn't figure out what technique to use. They kept on resetting themselves, and if I hadn't stopped the process, they probably would have shorted themselves out.

We also started studying what was keeping the moons in place. We could not push them any closer to each other; it was harder than we thought to move them. The space tug was able to give one a nudge away from the others, but after a day it had stopped and moved back in place. The scanner recorded nothing at all. I took one of the transported pieces and placed it outside the station to see if anything would happen. It didn't move. We tried to break off a chunk of the moon to study it in the lab, but nothing we tried could penetrate the material. We even tried energy weapons, but all they did was polish the surface where they hit and about ten meters beyond.

We ended up using the transporter to beam material around a section, to get a sample. But we didn't get any new answer.

Maybe if we'd had better scanners, we could have learned more. The only way to get them was with the technology of the First Ones.

"The repair drone has finished repairing what it can, and the ships are responding to my commands and have allowed me total access to all systems; we can now get to work,"

CHAPTER FIVE

The First Ones

At first it was slow, but after a couple of eye-openers, we started to learn a lot faster from the First Ones' cargo ships, in hope of bettering some of the technology we had. It took us two years. The work was hard, but those two years told us a lot. We may even have learned more in those last two years than in all the previous years. Once Athena got past a few somewhat incredible pieces of science, she took off. She could now translate the First Ones'ships' database with incredible speed. She tried to keep me up to speed, but with some of the things she was trying to teach me, it was like someone trying to teach the most advanced math formula to a ten-year-old. I wanted to learn, but it was beyond my capabilities.

It took us another four years to make advancements and improve everything. The scanners, transporters, and replicator became lot more efficient, and engines and power sources grew smaller and more powerful. We were even able to improve shields, force fields, damping fields, and artificial gravity. Athena also updated our star chart with the First Ones' chart. There were a lot more civilizations than the others knew about. Athena also learned that the First Ones could be the civilization that had put up the warnings and that would enforce them. The others never knew or even had seen them, but the old stories were that an old race would enforce the peace between the planets. When a battle was going to take place, both sides would lose power and find themselves back in their own space, far from each other. Other stories told that they would find a primitive race that had received a warning not to visit. They would lose power, find themselves elsewhere, and not remember or have data about where they had been. This all happened in the last five thousand years, after these ships came into the Nebula, but their technology was the only thing that could have done this. Maybe they had something to do with no ships having come in the past two hundred years. I hoped we would find out.

Athena did combine the transporter and replicator more efficiently. The transporters got better and better, and we could now build, repair, and replace anything using the transporter–replicator. I could make anything I wanted, quickly and with relatively little power. The really complex things were a little harder, as long as we had the raw material to start with, but that was the case with everything that was replicated. The complex things—like the memory core shell and fluid, and God's metal—could be made only a small amount at a time. Athena could design something that wasn't too big or too complex, and with the new transporter-replicator, it would just appear. The small complex things would just fade into existence.

One of the other things that we improved was the personnel transporters. I now could be transported in a nanosecond to anywhere in the nebula, if it wasn't too close to the radiation field (Athena set a limit of two AU, just to play it safe.) She still could, if needed, place an environmental suit on me if I was outside or on a derelict ship. There was no noise, no sparkly effect. I could snap my fingers and that one snap could be heard in both places. One might say I was in two places at the same time for an instant, which took a bit of getting used to, as I could see two separate places at the same instant. I just blinked and it was over.

Athena completely built a whole new station—more ship than station, really—around one of the memory cores. The station also had a four-meter-thick hull of God's metal. The shape of the station was a cylinder eleven hundred meters long and three hundred fifty meters in diameter. The station had an instrumentless bridge; the bridge would be an oblate sphere about ten meters in diameter with a command chair on a small platform raised in the center—nothing else. The inside wall of the bridge was the viewscreen, and Athena controlled everything and projected all visual aids on the screen. I just asked, and she did it; and most of the time I didn't have to ask. All the working decks were perpendicular to the memory core, but the living quarters were parallel, which left the rest of the station, a substantial portion of the inside of the ship, open.

So we made a forest. There was an area fifty meters from the inside of the hull to the core, so we put in trees (including some fruit trees), berry bushes, and even a garden. I wanted to see how real the plants Athena made with the replicators could be. Boy, did it work;

everything was real. The fruit and vegetables were good too. It took less than five minutes to build the ecosystem. We had a copy of the library of congress on its own big hard drive and, I had another big hard drive that had a DNA library on it that had been on the *Aegis* that Athena had transferred to her new hardware. With her new abilities, she was able to materialize a full-grown plant or one at any stage, and it would be alive instantly.

To go from the work area to the forest, I had to go through the living area. For Athena, she just had to go through a couple of hatches. I had to use a special entrance to go from one area of gravity to the other.

My living quarters were just a bedroom and a bath. We place something like a patio just outside my bedroom in the forest, with table and a chair to have my meals at. Otherwise I spent my time in the lab with Athena.

The new station had been built with the new builder drones. We used the replicator ship to build a frame dry dock that incorporated the transporter–replicator arrays to build the builder drones. Athena had built quite a few builder drones. These new builder drones were twice the size of NASA's space shuttle, had their own transporter–replicator that could adapt itself to do anything, and could link themselves to each other to build very large objects, such as this station. Half the builder drones hovered just centimeters from the surface of the moon and linked to their counterparts to form a circle three hundred fifty-one meters in diameter. The moon builder drones would start to dematerialize the moon's material, and then the other builder drones would start to rematerialize the God's Metal hull. It looked as if a hull was emerging from the ring of the builder drones while they were moving. At one end of the ship,

Athena had something like a hatch—a giant screw-in plug that could be removed to move the memory core in and out once we finished building the new station.

The scanner arrays were all over this station and had to be directly connected to the instruments on the inside because the hull interfered with the signal a lot. To get a clear scan, a direct connection was needed. A new type of microconnector was developed; an element that could be interwoven into the hull was found and used during materialization of the hull. We had thousands of connectors implemented into the hull. This also aided in the transporting of everything.

The scanners now could see everything inside the Nebula—and I mean everything. We discovered that the Nebula's radiation-free area was composed mostly of hydrogen, carbon dioxide, Nitrogen, and a forth unknown element that none of the civilizations recognized, and there were very large quantities of all these elements. Now I had an endless supply of water and air. My atmosphere generators were more efficient than plants at converting carbon dioxide to oxygen and combining hydrogen and oxygen to make water.

I could scan any ship and see every detail of it, including the First Ones' ship, even with their shields up. That meant I could transport onto the ship or transport anything off the ship even when its shields were up. With the new scanners and transporter, I no longer needed weapons; I could tell when a ship was getting ready to fire and beam a critical part of its weaponry out, making it unable to fire, and then beam out a part of its shield generator, causing it to be defenseless.

I put my theory to the test, giving the warship a set of the most advanced shields and having it target the old space station.

"Athena, as soon as you detect that the ship is energizing its weapon to fire, engage."

I gave the okay to the warship.

"Engaging," Athena said. A second later, she stated, *"The warship has emergency power only; shields, weapons, engines, communications, and main power are all disabled."*

We tried it several times with the warship and a couple of the other advanced ships; Athena didn't fail once.

We tried our luck with the scanners and looked toward the barrier. We still couldn't see into the barrier, though. We then looked at the moons and could see only a hundred meters into the moons, but I could now scan up to a meter into the transported God's Metal. However, I could lock onto only the first ten centimeters of it with the transporters. Now I could build things with the transporter, but not all at once; it was more like 3-D printing—one layer at a time. I could also see the molecules of the God's Metal before and after transporting. I could now see all the layer of the electrons and the nucleus, whereas previously I couldn't see the nucleus, because of the tightly packed layers of electrons. We still couldn't explain the metal's lack of mass.

We could scan the memory cores, and that was something, but some of the base elements were too complex to replicate, because some of the elements were unavailable, so if I wanted to replicate something like the shell or the fluid, I couldn't. I could reform the shell, but to do so I would have to use our extra containers. As for the fluid, we could only transport it. I did find out the memory size; one core could hold a little over forty-one million cubic meters of the fluid, which I called liquid memory, and each cubic meter of liquid memory could hold a billion domegemegrottebytes (that's a quantity of bytes totaling one with forty-five zeros following it), for a grand total of bytes equating to forty-one followed by fifty-four zeros, and we had sixteen of them. We found out how to hook them up, and man could it take on data fast—even for Athena.

Even most of the power systems of the alien's ships were pretty advanced; some had been running a long time and were running out of power. We were able to recharge most of them by building power stations that used the solar power of the Nebula to provide power to some of the ships. The ones we couldn't recharge we were able to use the technology of the First Ones' more advanced power system to modify.

The engines were the icing on the cake. It was like having a shuttlecraft engine with the power of a warship. The size of the engine on the First Ones' cargo ships were unreal. At first we thought that the main engines had been jettisoned and these were only maneuvering engines. We knew they were advanced, but not *that* advanced. It took Athena six months to figure out the technology. Once she figured it out, she could have easily modified the other engines, but there was no need to at the time.

My environmental suit was something else. It was skin tight, which wasn't too flattering, and was only four millimeters thick, with an energy shield that would allow me to be shot by an Abrams tank and not feel it; the projectile would more than likely be flattened and then fall away, the suit and shields absorbing the energy. There was a utility belt with a power pack, an atmosphere generator, a communicator, a transporter–replicator, and a medical kit, each device no bigger than a cell phone. The suit also had maneuvering thrusters, and a backpack with essentials element in case of emergencies.

With all the improvements done, the new station complete, and the new science learned, we were ready to go back to the barrier, but first we had to build more probes.

With the help of the First Ones' engines, Athena was able to design a new engine. It had three main components: the power source, the converter, and the emitter. The emitter could be interwoven into the outer layer of the hull at the leading and trailing edges of the probe.

With all the advancements and improvements we had made, we knew we should be able to figure something out with the barrier. With all the databases available, we tried to find out what kind of radiation we'd had on *Aegis* when we jumped, but our instruments were so primitive that we couldn't duplicate our findings well enough to compare them. Since none of the other civilizations had experimented with folding space, we couldn't theorize on how to make the radiation.

With the new station, we can better explore the barrier. Athena was able to move around this station just as easily as the old one and even into the ecosystem. She could operate everything from wherever she was in the new station. She stayed in constant communication with me in the instrumentless bridge, but I still felt uneasy about it. I had an earpiece that helped a little.

For a couple of months, we were building probes. We built twenty-one probes using God's Metal for their hulls, some with one-meter-thick hulls, some with ten-meter-thick hulls, and some with hundred-meter-thick hulls. We used the Gato-size probes from the first visit to the barrier as a model. We stretched out the inner diameter to sixteen meters with new scanners, computers, power sources, and other upgraded equipment, and we began to build them using the frame space dock we had used to create the builder drones. We made three at a time. Then we used the builder drones to apply the hulls to the probes, just as we had done to the station. Building the hundred-meter hulls probes was slow—slower than building the station—and just like the station's hull, the probes' hulls had microconnectors too. Two each of the ten-meter and hundred-meter hull probes were mechanical, with mechanical components and chemical rockets boosters. The ten-meter probes had four boosters, and the hundred-meter probes had eight. The boosters on the hundred-meter probes were massive. The boosters on the ten-meter probes were one hundred meters long by thirty meters in diameter; the ones on the hundred-meter probes were three hundred meters long by sixty meters in diameter. We hoped the radiation would not interfere with the rockets' fuel, since we did not use God's Metal for the booster hulls.

The scanners' receiving antennas were imbedded in the forward parts of the probes with three quarters of a meter of God's Metal on the outer surface and three shields on the inner side to help keep the scanners working for as long as possible. They could see only twenty million kilometers, but that was good enough for the test. The very thin conduit that went from the antennas to the instruments was interwoven in such a way that it needed only 18 percent more God's Metal on the inside to make up what was needed to maintain the density of the hull.

Just as we were about to leave, we decided to build one more hundred-meter-hull probe, but this was designed to try to capture some of the barrier. It hadn't gone too well the last time, but I thought that maybe with the God's Metal it would work this time.

We went back to the barrier and spent the next six months with the new probes that had the God's Metal hulls. The first one-meter-hull probe showed the slowest penetration of all the previous hulls—a lot slower. It just barely penetrated the barrier. We also noticed that the radiation field area was still trying to completely penetrate the God's Metal hull but was slowed down quite a bit. Given it time, it would penetrate it. Nothing seemed to stop it; even the radiation we had encountered in the jumps was consumed by it. We decided to keep everything out of the radiation field until necessary.

The other one-meter-hull probes weren't used. We sent them back to the staging area. We would figure out what to do with them later.

The first three ten-meter-hull probes penetrated the barrier by one hundred thousand kilometers and were immediately pushed back out. We tried to determine whether the probes could see each other inside the barrier, but no luck—they couldn't. For the next launch, we used a mechanical ten-meter-hull probe. It penetrated the barrier and went well beyond, but we couldn't scan how much farther the probe traveled. Once it entered the barrier, we lost track of it. Even using the first three ten-meter-hull probes to track it, the data we later retrieved showed that it traveled about four hundred thousand kilometers into the barrier and recorded the rate of resistance. Next we launched two hundred-meter-hull probes. Both probes entered the barrier using standard engines at half the speed of light. The mechanical one traveled twenty-five million kilometers into the barrier, and the other probe only twenty million kilometers. The rate of resistance was the same until the mechanical one got to about twenty-two million kilometers, and then the rate of resistance increased by a factor of ten. We also noticed that not all the fuel was used up; the boosters had anywhere from 10 to 18 percent of their fuel remaining.

We refueled the mechanical probe and used the standard probe to tow the mechanical probe as far as twenty million kilometers and then launch it. When we retrieved both probes, we found that not all of the mechanical probe's boosters had ignited. Somehow the radiation had kept some of the igniters from firing, and those that had fired hadn't stayed lit for very long.

Athena had the builder drones build a huge single booster. It was five hundred meters long and seventy-five meters in diameter, with a removable nose cone and ten meters of God' metal for the hull. It was almost as big as the Sea Dragon. We strapped on the mechanical and standard probes to the booster. The standard probe was designed to break away once it entered the barrier, and it would ignite just before entering the barrier. The mechanical probe traveled about forty-million kilometers. We noticed that it burned all of its fuel.

We had the booster refilled and attached to the first mechanical probe; then we had a second booster built and attached the other mechanical probe to it. The first booster nose cone was removed, and we placed a modified adapter to attach the second booster (it would be like a second stage); the first stage would ignite it like on the model rockets I built when I was a kid. Then we added two standard probes near the attachment point to take this makeshift super probe to the edge of the barrier, where the first booster would ignite. When the first booster got to the end of its fuel, the second booster would ignite—I hoped.

When we retrieved the mechanical probes, the first one worked but the second one failed to launch because the radiation had penetrated the second's booster and disrupted everything, including the mechanical components, before it could launch, so we wouldn't have gotten anything anyway.

We sent the hundred-meter probe that was built to capture some of the barrier to the very edge of the barrier. It maneuvered its nose into the barrier and opened the door to flood the interior with the barrier. It then closed its door, but once the barrier entered the interior, everything failed. The radiation hadn't penetrated the hull all the way, so we knew we should have some time. After we got it back to the station and out of the radiation field, and just as we crossed the threshold, everything came back online. We hooked up to the scanner connectors, but the scanners saw nothing. So we opened the doors, and there was nothing inside. The seal was airtight. The interior of the probe was clean—no radiation at all—but it hadn't captured any radiation—not even to study for a few seconds. It should have, but the instruments had failed. With that much of the radiation in the interior, there should have been some trace, as we had quickly retrieved it. This was another mystery of the barrier.

We tried a high-speed approach and got one of standard probes to go faster than light speed and enter the barrier. It made it to forty-five million kilometers. We found out that in the last five million kilometers, the resistance became stable. So we tried it at twice the speed of light. It didn't get as far; it barely made it to forty million kilometers. We tried further at various speeds. Our attempts right at light speed got the best results.

We tried the light-speed testing of the barrier at several various locations just to make sure there wasn't a weak spot. We retrieved enough data to determine that we were close to the edge of the barrier maybe another ten million kilometers. That meant the barrier could be at least fifty-five million kilometers wide.

We also found out that engine emitters were not affected by the radiation like everything else was, so the blisters were at the right thickness. The radiation affected the power source, which caused the engines to shut down. What we thought would not be affected but was affected by the barrier was God's Metal. When the probes went into the barrier, their surfaces became very glossy, the transporter could no longer lock on to them, and the scanner could no longer see the God's Metal, and magnification was useless. All we could see was a reflection. Since the transporter could no longer lock on to them, they could not be reused for building material. But the radiation still did not adhere to the God's Metal.

With all this data, we went back to the staging area. Athena and I started going over everything. Since we had only estimated the thickness of the barrier at a little over fifty million kilometers, we took the precaution of assuming that the barrier was two hundred million kilometers thick and agreed that a thousand-meter hull should be more than enough to get us through the barrier. We hoped the radiation would penetrate only 50 percent of the hull if we could get through it fast enough. None of the ships were able to get an accurate reading of the size of the Nebula before they entered it.

During all this time, Athena made sure I was on a regular schedule. After supper, I would spend time in the forest for relaxation. She kept me on a work schedule of less than eight hours per day. I was getting old, and I started getting tired more frequently.

CHAPTER SIX

Designing the Ship

Athena and I started thinking about the shape of the ship. I always liked the stingray-style Martian war machine from the 1953 science fiction movie *War of the Worlds*, so we used that as the basis of the design. We needed the ship to get us out of the Nebula and have the hull a thousand meters thick, so that would make it enormous.

"The first thing we need is a computer room to house your sphere and the sixteen memory cores," I said. "That would make the room twenty-two hundred and fifty meters wide, and just as long, by one thousand meters high. I think we should put the cores in four rows of four with two hundred fifty meters in between them and the walls, and have you between the second and third rows in the center of the room—on a platform, maybe. You can decide on that later when you're building it."

"Okay, I will think about it," Athena responded.

"The computer room will go on the center of the forward wall of the cargo hold, with alcoves or something on the forward wall serving as places to put an instrumentless bridge, living quarters, that new medical bay you've been working on, and whatever else I need."

We also agreed that the computer room—or building, since it was bigger than any buildings on Earth—should be built first and should be self-sufficient.

"We will need to add a basement to house all the machinery and equipment for everything," Athena said. *"All exterior walls and the floors and ceilings would be made of God's Metal at least ten meters thick, with another material on the surfaces of the floors, because otherwise it would be like trying to walk on polished glass."*

"With it being so light and so strong, you wouldn't need to use any interior support beams or columns," I said. "It should have no doors or hatches leading out of it. We could have a hatch leading to the basement. It should be about sixteen meters square and should be like an elevator on an aircraft carrier. The interior height of the basement should be about twenty meters. The width and length would be the same as the computer room. There would be a lot of unused space—a little over three quarters of it. We could put stuff in there that we find once we get out of here."

"I can have a buffer shield over the scanner connector to allow only our transporter to beam into or out of the ship."

"Secondly, we need a cargo hold to put all the ships in … But that won't work. The ship would be the size of a moon; that would take too long to build."

"And use more power then what we have to build with."

"So," I said, "we put the ships in four categories. The first category of ships comprises all the really old ships that are derelict. We will have all their data retrieved; a digital copy of the complete ship will be made, and then they will be transported down to their base elements to help build the ship. The second category would be the ships that aren't that complex and can be kept in the transporter's buffer; we can partition part of the memory core we are using. The third category would be the rest of the ships except the ten very large ships that we would have to tow, and that would be the fourth category."

"To tow the ships," Athena said, *"we can build a temporary structure off the spine of Stingray big enough to attach the ships to."*

"The Star Ship *Stingray*—that sounds nice," I replied. "We should put the probes and boosters in the cargo ships or make them part of the structure, since we cannot transport them into *Stingray*."

"The cargo hold would be roughly nine thousand meters wide by fifteen thousand meters long, and fifteen hundred meters high, with a pit twenty-five hundred meters wide by ten thousand meters long and five hundred meters deep, and a raised ceiling just as wide as the pit by fifty-five hundred meters long and five hundred meters high. It also would have a lot of alcoves along the side in varies size and shapes. That should provide enough room to house all the category-three ships. The first stations and Aegis would be digitally copied and transported down to base elements after Stingray was built. For the second station, we would have to put the ecosystem in the transporter's buffer and

use God's Metal to help build Stingray if we have too, because we no longer need it."

"We really don't need it; you can put the forest elsewhere in the ship," I said.

"The third thing we need for the ship is an engine room. We have the calculation for the size of the cargo hold and the computer room, and I have come up with the size of the ship. It would have a wingspan of twenty-four thousand meters, and the body would be forty-five hundred meters high. To add the engine room that we need, we can design a tail that tapers out, making it look similar to a manatee's tail pointing straight out. The room only needs to be one thousand meters wide, two thousand meters long, and only twenty meters high to accommodate the engine's power source and convertor. The engine emitter would be interwoven in the trailing edge of the tail, like the probes. We also had to have something like a tunnel about four meters in diameter from the cargo hold out to the engine room. The overall length of Stingray would be thirty-seven thousand five hundred meters."

"The main scanner packet would need to be placed in the nose. We found a material from one of the really old ships that we could infuse with God's Metal; it materialized into a bright gold material that will be strong enough to make a dome big enough to cover the scanner antennas yet let them see through it, and it will help in emitting a deflector shield across the front of the ship."

"We should also place auxiliary scanners in the wing tips," I added, "and microscanners throughout the ship, the cargo hold, and the engine room, since the outside scanners couldn't see inside the ship. This way, Athena, you could see every inch of the inside. There should also be auxiliary engines in the leading and trailing edges of the wings, just in case. I can't wait until we get this built and get out of here to find out how fast it will go.

"The instrumentless bridge would have no door; the only way in or out would be the transporter, which would be almost anywhere in the ship, since there would be no doors. The bridge would only have a platform with no chair. I hardly ever use the chair in the bridge I have now. Everything will appear on the walls as a hologram in front of me. I like the current bridge, but I feel alone in it."

"My living quarters would be a one-bedroom apartment with the best kitchen I could dream up. It would also have a large screen to view movies in a living room. I have a lot of movies. I have been watching more of them lately on the patio. We would have to dim the light in the forest, but once I have the living room, we won't have to do that; it would be more like a theater. I might still have to watch movies in the forest, because of the drive-in theater effect; I do like that. I always liked that when I was a kid, and this reminded me how much I miss it."

We noticed that the fluid in the memory core that we had been using on the station to download all the data we had been gathering had started to glow. It was dim at first, but once all the data from all the ships were downloaded, it got a little brighter—not much, just a little. We barely had anything downloaded compared to its capacity.

Now we had the design of the ship worked out, knew the size of it, and had planned where everything was supposed to go. I decided that we had earned a day off, so I went out onto the deck at the edge of the forest and smelled the air.

"Athena, how about a gentle breeze?"

A breeze started up, rustling the trees.

"That's nice, just right. I think I'll take a nap. How about a nice, comfortable deck chair." A chair appeared, and I sat down on it, stretched out, and fell asleep.

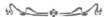

Athena was doing some final calculations on the ship in the lab when her med scanner that she had watching me all the time flashed "Alert." Before the alert finished flashing the first time, Athena had me in the new med bay in the diagnostic and treatment chamber. I was having a coronary artery spasm. From the time that it happened to within twenty heart beats, Athena had diagnosed and repaired my heart. Athena was just inside the doorway of her new med bay, because she would fill up the room if she came in any farther into the room. After Athena was satisfied I was okay, she had a force field very gently pick me up and put me on the monitoring bed.

As I was waking up, I noticed I was not on the deck chair in the forest anymore but rather on a medical bed in Athena's new medical bay. Athena angled the bed up so I could look around. The room was sixteen meters by twenty meters and about twelve meters high. To the right of me was a transparent cylinder three meters tall and about one and a half meters in diameter. Above and behind me on the wall was a screen that displayed my vitals. To my left was another bed a little bigger than this one that looked somewhat like a tanning bed.

"Athena, what's going on? Why am I here?" I asked, looking somewhat puzzled.

"You had a mild heart attack—nothing serious, but I had to take care of it right away."

I said, "I didn't feel anything."

"It was very mild, and I repaired your heart very quickly."

"I have been here almost thirty-two years in the Nebula. When I first got here, I was fifty; now I'm eighty-two years old. I feel good for being eighty-two, but I wonder how much longer this is going to last. Athena, you have kept me in very good health using the advancements in medicine you have discovered, and I want to thank you for all this."

I kept looking at what looked like a tanning bed. I had to ask.

"Athena, tell me that's not a tanning bed."

"No, it's not; it's a diagnostic and treatment chamber. I can use it to treat you for anything."

"Oh, from here it looks like a tanning bed. For a minute I thought you were beaming me down here while I was sleeping to get a tan. By the way, how have I been getting tanned?" I asked.

"I have modified the lights in the forest to tan you a little at a time. Remember: you haven't seen a sun in over thirty years. I have something to show you in this new medical bay and would like to talk to you about it."

For the past couple of years, Athena had been working on a new medical bay. It looked like a bank vault; the bay was completely surrounded with ten meters of God's Metal, and the door … wow.

"I have been developing a new medical processor. With these new advancements, I can actually reverse your age back to when you were at your prime simply by restoring your chromosomes. It will take some time, but it will also extend your life span quite a bit—I mean a very long time—and does not include the time you use for the process."

"The process?"

"The process is to place you in that tank, in a solution of highly charged, oxygen-rich plasma. Then all your chromosomes will be regenerated. You will be in suspended animation, and this will slow down your normal cell regeneration rate. A complete cycle of your cells will take two years. I need to do twenty cycles, making sure every other cycle that your chromosomes are all regenerated. So you will spend almost a hundred years—maybe more—in suspended animation."

"What will my life span be then?" I asked.

"A thousand years. Maybe more."

"A thousand year maybe more, wow, a thousand years—that's a long time. So it will take a hundred years for this process. I'll miss seeing the ship being built. But if I don't do this, I'll never see the ship built. Hey, maybe I can see one or more of the memory cores get filled up during my life span. Now I see the reason for the vault. I will be in here for a hundred years."

"Yes, and I want to make sure you are safe, as you say, just in case"

"Will there be any pain or any other ill effects?" I asked.

"There shouldn't be any during or after you get out of suspended animation, plus I might be able to grow your hair back and get rid of your potbelly you're always complaining about"

"Okay, that's good, but I would like to help you get started."

"There is one other thing I'd like to ask you. If I could keep you in another type of suspended animation to teach you most of this technology and show you the building of the ship, it would take you twenty years, but I assure you it will be well worth it."

"Okay, if it's not going to hurt or anything. Twenty out of a thousand is not long."

"It will be as if you were here watching the whole thing, and I may be able to communicate with you while you are under if everything goes right."

"That will be interesting."

"You must take it easy from now on. No more spacewalks or trips into the field."

"No more spacewalks, man ... what a bummer."

"Okay, you can go on a few spacewalks, but not to work."

"Let's see *Stingray*. Please put it right here in front of me," I said. A hologram appeared. "Thank you. That looks great. Wow, and that's a little over thirty-seven thousand meters long; that's big. Could you please bring up the ships we are going to tow with the tow structure?" The holographic *Stingray* moved forward a little, and the other ships appeared with the tow structure. "So this is what it's supposed to look like."

"Yes, as of right now."

We started moving the station and all the ships that were needed close to the moons, since we were going to use the moons for the bulk of the resources to build the structure of *Stingray*. We were going to keep the fifteen memory cores in their cradles in the First Ones' ship's cargo holds until they were needed and use the ship's power sources. We would use one ship at a time. When each got down to 20 percent, we would switch to another ship. The previous ship would then regenerate, so by the time the fourth ship got down to 20 percent, the first one would be back up to full power. Thus we could use the ships ten times before any major maintenance needed to be done.

Athena had discovered a way to build several power stations near the radiation field to get power from the solar rays and gravity waves of the Nebula. Between the station and the ships, we had enough power to build the ship.

We transported all the base elements into cubes or used force fields to hold them together and used cargo ships to place them. We had to spread the ship out, because some of the element could not get close to each other. It took almost three months to get everything ready and build two thousand of the builder drones, Athena would need more later and would continue building them. Once she started building the main hull, she will need another four thousand, maybe more.

The moon we had been removing all the God's Metal from would be the first moon we would start on.

I walked into the new medical bay, and the big door closed behind me and clamps locked it into place.

"Athena, I have to tell you I'm a little scared about this. But I trust you, so let's do this. A hundred twenty years, huh? No more. Okay. Wait a minute; that means I will be over two hundred years old when I wake up."

"Don't worry; I won't let anything happen to you. If anything did, I would be alone, and that scares me. You will soon be a thirty-year-old who is over two hundred years old. I hope."

"You hope! Great, now she's developing a sense of humor."

I lay down on the medical bed that looked like a tanning bed. It was actually a medical array bed. A warm field came slowly over me. The lights dimmed a little, and I fell asleep … I think.

CHAPTER SEVEN

Waking up

I opened my eyes and looked around. I was still in the medical bay but was hovering above the floor, off to the side of the bay where I saw the tube. *Wait a minute; I'm in the tube.* I saw that I was in liquid. Just before I could panic, a voice in my head said, *Calm.* I think it was in my head, anyhow. Then it said, *Sleep,* and I fell asleep. I think I woke up, but I was floating in space. I felt fine, and then all these things started to appear: formulas, molecules, charts, graphs, and other stuff that started to make sense. I started to catch on to what was happening. I was learning new things. Then something appeared—a great big green box. *Wait, it's the computer room.* Then another form started to emerge around the computer room and take shape. The *Stingray* was being built. Then it was finished. It was one hell of a ship. Next I was standing on the top of the computer room, at the edge, looking at the cargo hold. *Wow, is this place big.*

Then it started to fill up with ships. Soon there was hardly any room left. Now I was flying in between the ships to the back of the hold to the tunnel, and then down the tunnel to the engine room. *Wow, that was cool.* This was the engine room, and there was the engine. it sure didn't look big enough to power the ship at high speeds.

Then all faded to dark and slowly lit up again. I was standing among pillars. *Wait, those are the memory cores. This is the computer room. Man, this place is massive, and so are these memory cores.* I looked at the front wall, and about twenty meters from the floor was a deck containing the med bay, the bridge, and my apartment. I flew around the room, seeing everything. I landed on the elevator, and it lowered down to the so-called basement. Sure enough, over three-quarters of it was empty. I flew back up to the center of the computer room, and everything faded again.

Next I awoke on the diagnostic bed. I was a little dizzy, I heard someone say, *"Are you dizzy? Relax and take a few deep breaths. That's it. Breathe deeply."*

I opened my eyes and saw that I was on the diagnostic bed.

"Athena?"

"Yes, I am here."

"You sound a little different. Did everything go okay? Are you okay? Is the ship finished? Did anything bad happen? Hey, is that you? Are you floating? You are."

"Yes, everything is okay, including me, and yes, the ship is complete. And no, nothing bad happened. Here is a status report. The ship is complete. All systems are 100 percent. The scanners work as expected, and so do the engines. We are in the ship, opening the door. All the ships that needed to be placed in the cargo hold are in. The tow structure is in place with the ten ships hooked up, waiting to transport the remaining ships that are to be transported into the buffer. All but a hundred builder drones have

been transported back to base elements. The builder drones that are left are stowed in the tow structure. We had to store all the cargo we have left, which is about 18 percent of what we had in the cargo ship. Most of the cargo holds on the ships are full. Stingray has no cargo space left because of the ships." There was a moment of silence, and then she continued. *"Now for the update on you. You have 10 percent body fat, like you asked."*

"Wow. Hey, I have a full head of hair," I said with a little excitement.

"Yes, and I was able to get rid of all of the other body hair except your eyebrows. If you want to grow a beard or a mustache, I can help you grow them. You are six times stronger than most athletic humans. I increased your bone and muscle density. You have perfect sight and hearing. You have total memory recall. Your ability to learn has increased tenfold, maybe more, and so has your ability to heal." She paused momentarily. *"And I have increased your lifespan to four thousand years, maybe more, and I can repeat the process at least five times."*

"What? Wow! Four thousand years and five times? That's twenty thousand years. Wow, that's a long time. Twenty thousand years … I can't … that's a little hard to take in. Twenty thousand years. It may take that long to get home."

"No, it won't take us that long, but we may need twenty thousand years to explore the galaxy. If the engines perform the way they should, we can be home in almost six years. According to the First Ones, this is the oldest part of the galaxy, but they have not gotten to our part of it, at the time of these ships. So we may need to take our time getting home."

"You bet we are going to take our time getting home. I want to see some of these places."

The bed angled up to where I was almost vertical. I stepped onto the floor, and I could feel a field holding me.

"I have adjusted the gravity, so you can start walking around again, and I'm holding you up with a force field. You need to learn to walk again while I adjust the gravity back up to one G. This could take a couple of hours. But first I want you to drink something."

A glass appeared in front of me. I grabbed it and started drinking. "This tastes like tomato juice."

"Yes, it is supposed to, but it's more than just tomato juice. It's a lot of protein, vitamins, and minerals to help you get started."

It took me only an hour to learn to walk again, but it wore me out. I may have been strong, but being just out of suspended animation, I would have to work on my stamina to get it equal to my strength.

"Athena, I need a full-length mirror please." A two-meter-tall sheet of mirrored glass appeared in front of me. "Thank you. Hey, I have six-pack abs … Never had that before. No hair … okay. I never looked this good in my prime. How hard is it going to be to maintain this fitness?"

"Your metabolism will be easy to control with the food and supplements we have."

A chair appeared along with a table topped with clothing. I put on the clothes; they were different.

"Athena, they're softer than my other clothes. What's different about them?"

"I have improved your environmental suit. It incorporates a field generator and transporter-replicator to instantly detect your environment and adapt to it."

"So this is a uniform. And are these shoes or socks?"

"They are both, sort of, and they also can adapt to your environment and adjust to it. Now, I wanted to make sure you were all right before I started beaming the ships into the buffer. Is it okay to start?"

"Oh yes, go right ahead. Would you please show me *Stingray*?"

The lights dimmed a little, and a holographic model of *Stingray* appeared in front of me. I could turn it to all different angles. It was jade green with a gold nose and wing tips. I placed it back in front of me at eye level.

"Athena, would you please show me *Stingray* with the tow structure and the other ships."

Now the holograph of *Stingray* was floating in front of me with the tow structure with the ships tethered to it. The tow structure was a framed structure like the space dry dock we used to build the builder drones, plus I noticed that she had incorporated the boosters into the frame. The ships were in two rows. The structure not only went down in between them but also around each of them, so they were tethered on all sides. The largest ship was the first one on the left; it was over six kilometers long. It was a cargo ship, and it looked like a Typhoon-class sub with no conning tower and with eight massive engines at the tail of it. It was empty when it entered the Nebula; it was also the second-to-last ship to enter the Nebula, and now it had all the probes in it.

To the right of it was a hospital ship and some sort of passage ship. Together they equaled the length of the giant cargo ship. They were each about two and half kilometers long. The hospital ship was the last ship to enter the Nebula. The passage ship had entered about three thousand years ago. Its cabins were all the same, with no different classes—not even for the crew. It also had livestock stalls next to each cabin. The number of cabins and stalls were equal. Each member had what looked like a dragon, according to the ship's database. The database contained everything about the ship's home civilization. Their world had been dying, so they had left. It also mentioned other ships. I hoped they had made it.

The next two in line were the replicator and mining ships next to each other. They were from the same civilization and had been on their way home when they took a shortcut through the Nebula. They were also about three kilometers long. They entered the nebula about fifteen hundred years ago. The container ships were with them. Athena was able to put them in the transporter buffer. They were the ones that had the black goo replicators and the liquid atmospheres.

The next in line were the four First Ones' ships. They were in two rows of two. They were just over two kilometers long each. They didn't like being tethered, and parts of their computer cores had to be deactivated.

The last ship was an old tanker. The only reason it didn't get copied and turned into base elements was that it was almost a piece of art; it was unique. It was about eighteen hundred meters long and very elegant for a tanker

"Hmm, you couldn't justify saving the station," I said.

"I'm afraid not. The tow structure with these many ships has me a little concerned. If the barrier is over a hundred million kilometers, the tow structure could be damaged. I used the station's God's metal to help build the computer room, but I did transport the forest to its own buffer, and once all the ships are out of the cargo hold, I will build a biosphere on top of the computer room if you would like."

"That would be nice, maybe with a track ... Wait a minute; I don't like jogging. Maybe with a pond, so I can go fishing or swimming. Speaking of the computer room, I want to go see it. So I just step out this door ..." And there it was. Wow, what a sight.

CHAPTER EIGHT

Athena's Upgrades

"*Yes, go onto the deck and you can see the whole room,*" Athena said.

I stepped out onto the deck. "Wow. I am about ready to call this nebula the Wow Nebula; ever since I got here, I've been saying 'wow' a lot, and I have a feeling I'm going to keep on saying it a lot."

This room was over 1,250 acres and a thousand meters high. There were the memory cores—all sixteen of them. They looked like giant towers holding up the sky. The entire ceiling was illuminated; it was not too bright, but bright enough so I could see everything. The cores had power to them and looked alive. The blue liquid was churning very slowly; I had to stare at it to see it move—except the two closest ones. Those two I could easily see moving. Those were the ones we were using. The med bay, the bridge, and my living quarters were on this deck, which protruded from the forward wall about forty meters and twenty meters from the floor of the computer room. The color of the walls was jade green, and the floor was grey-green with gold pathways leading to and from the memory cores. The pathways were about ten meters wide. The med bay was made of jade-green God's Metal, and the bridge and my living quarters were bright gray. "This room is huge; I could fly a plane in here. Hey, I wonder ... no, I'd better not," I said with a little excitement. Athena's sphere came gliding up next to me on the deck, and I got my first really good look at her.

"Wow. See; I'm not the only one that got the upgrades. Look at you. You're sort of blue. Is that lightning in there?"

Athena has a new sphere, its eight-meter diameter was just a little smaller than the old one. Her outer surface was made up of the transparent material of the memory core's shell; she had used the shell of the liquid memory containers and their fluid. I could see the liquid memory underneath the shell; and what else was in there I don't know, but the fluid was moving and changing shades of blue. Lightning bolts were running through her—some long ones and some short ones. There was no visible maneuvering thruster, but she floated and moved. I put my hand on her to push and said, "You're warm." She was very easy to move. She came back to position silently and just hovered there.

"I designed and built my new sphere and then transported myself into it," she said. *"It was actually very easy. I have my own transporter inside me now. I can go anywhere I want, and I am able to travel at high speeds. I also have my own scanners and field and gravity generators, and so far I have been able to look inside the data cores in all the computers here very easily without them knowing it. I can't wait to get out of here to see if I can talk to other ships."*

I could feel her presence, her warmth, but there was no sound, no vibration. She could pick things up and turn them around with some kind of field. She looked like one of those static electricity balls without a center. My hand generated little lightning bolts, but it wasn't static electricity.

"Hey, is that *Aegis*? You didn't take *Aegis* down to base elements?"

"Yes, that's Aegis. No I couldn't take Aegis down to base elements, just in case something was to happen. But I did give Aegis some upgrades also. I removed the gimbal rings; replaced the engines; replaced the recycling machine with a replicator; installed shields, artificial gravity generators, scanners, an atmosphere, field generators, a transporter, a new and more powerful power source, and a computer system that's better than any of these ships have—but not as good as me."

"How fast will *Aegis* go? Oh, wait; can we use a warp chart to track our speed?"

"Yes, if you wish. The original or the revised one?"

"Let's use the original one for now. How fast can you go?"

"With standard shields, I can go to warp seven. With high-velocity shields, I can get up to warp ten."

"What time is it? I'm a little tried. Let's see my quarters."

I appeared in the living room.

"It's twenty-two hundred hours," Athena said, *"and here is your living room. You can stretch out on the sofa and watch your movies on this large viewscreen."*

"Large" was right. It was six meters by six meters. The room was six meters cubed, with perfect acoustics. Looking back at the screen, on the left wall was one large doorway that was in the middle of the wall, leading to the kitchen and to the dining room. The kitchen and dining room were open to each other and were the same length and width as the living room. The forward wall had a double oven and a range top and a large double sink about three-quarters of a meter away on the countertop that encompassed the kitchen half of the room, except where the double oven was. Why? Because I wanted them. The wall opposite the doorway was another doorway going into the bedroom. This doorway was just as large as the other. The bedroom was an appropriate size to have a queen-size bed with plenty of room around it; the bed was against the back wall, and there was nothing else in the room, as there was no need for now. The doorway to the bathroom was across from the bedroom doorway. The bathroom was also a decent size, with the sink and vanity opposite the doorway. There was a very large mirror, with the toilet to the left and a shower to the right.

As I walked to the bedroom, Athena had a glass of tomato juice on the counter for me. I drank it, went to the bedroom, took off my clothes, and climbed into bed. "Ah, I like this bed," I said as I fell asleep.

CHAPTER NINE

The Escape

As I got up in early morning, the lights came on and started to get bright.

"Athena, what time is it?"

"It's 0-four hundred."

"I had only six hours of sleep. It was a good sleep, and I'm not tired. Is this going to be the norm?"

"Unknown. You are no longer normal. You have been in suspended animation for a hundred twenty years, and your lifespan is now at four thousand years plus. I suggest we see what happens in the next few weeks and make adjustments then."

"Okay, we will start off using a standard day clock and, like you said, see what happens."

I got out of bed and walked into the bathroom. "I love these heated floors," I said as I looked into the mirror. I picked up the bottle of rinse. No more brushing my teeth; I would just use this rinse and be done until evening.

"So no shaving—good. I just rinse my mouth, pee in the toilet, and I'm done. I like this." I walked out of the bathroom.

"I can upgrade your toilet."

"Oh no, I don't like those space toilets. This is one thing we won't change".

I made my way to the kitchen. Athena had my breakfast waiting for me at the table—a tall glass of that tomato juice, which wasn't bad at all, some scrambled eggs, and a couple of links of sausage.

"Athena, what's with the tomato juice? Is there something I should know?" I asked as I drank it down. "It's pretty good anyway."

"It's a protein, vitamin, and mineral drink that you will need for the next two days for breakfast and in the evening. It will help your system get to a somewhat normal state after being in suspended animation for all those years. All ships have been beamed into the buffer; we are ready."

"Okay, that was good. Beam me to the bridge, and let's get this show on the road."

I appeared on the bridge. What appeared around me was the space outside. I was standing where *Stingray* was, and I could see all around. I look down and saw the moons—the ones that were left. I looked behind me and could see the tow structure with the ten ships.

"Athena, we are ready to go right."

"Yes, all systems are checked out and everything is go."

As I looked around trying to figure out where to look for Athena, I said, "Athena, you can project this hologram anywhere. I really don't like being in here. Are you down on the floor?"

"Yes, I'm in the center of the computer room," Athena responded.

"Good. Beam me down next to you." In the blink of an eye, I was standing next to Athena. "That's better. Now put the hologram around us. This is more like it. I never felt right being in that type of bridge by myself."

Yes, I noticed something was making you nervous. At first I thought it was because you were in a confined space, and I was going to suggest a larger bridge.

"That was sort of it, but mostly it was trying to talk to you. I just don't like talking to air; this is better."

"Enough of that. Let's get started. Proceed to the barrier, and let's see if we can get out of here."

Aye aye, sir. Proceeding to the barrier. It's 0-five hundred hours.

It took us eleven and half hours to get to the edge of the radiation field. We traveled just under the speed of light, using barely any engine power. That was about as fast as we should should have gone with the tow structure and ships.

About six hours into the first leg, I said, "Athena, may I have a hoagie and a soda? I'm getting a little hungry."

Sure. Would you like to go to your dining room?

"No. Could I have a table and chair placed here to eat?" A table and chair appeared. "Thank you."

After I was finished with my hoagie, I said, "Athena, that was good, thank you. You can take the table and chair, but I'll keep my glass. Would you refill it for me please?" As I looked at my glass and saw it fill back up, I thought to myself that I had gotten one of those magician's glasses that refilled itself. "Thank you."

Just as we started to enter the radiation field, Athena informed me, *We should reduce speed to 40 percent of light speed.*

"Okay. I guess now is an appropriate time to go eat supper, but first let's see how everything is going."

"All systems are go. The shield is holding up against the radiation as expected. The damping and structure fields on the tow structure are holding, shutting down all ships. We should reach the barrier in thirty-three hours."

"What time is it now?"

"It's eighteen hundred hours."

Athena transported me to my dining room. I grabbed the chair and sat down in it.

"What would you like for dinner?"

"I think I'll start with a small salad with Thousand Island dressing and that tomato drink, and then I'll have a small steak, medium rare, with mushroom and brown gravy; a small baked potato with lots of butter; sautéed green beans; and a cold tall glass of that lager we came up with, with ice crystals in it. Could you please play my playlist of seventies rock? Thank you."

Just as I asked for it, it would appear in front of me, and the music would come out of the air as usual. As I finished my meal, I told Athena, "That was perfect—just what I needed after a long winter's nap."

"Some nap—a one-hundred-twenty-year nap. How do you feel?"

"I feel great—better than I have in a long time. Why do you need to run a med scan on me?" I said.

"I have run a med scan on you constantly since I had access to the scanners."

"Okay, keeping a watchful eye on me, huh? That's okay. Would you beam me back down to the floor with you?"

As I appeared on the floor next to Athena, she brought up the hologram and continued my music.

"Okay, that's a whole lot of pink nothing. Could I get a chair please? Thank you."

For the next four hours, I sat there listening to my music and looking at the pink nothing.

"You know something? I think I need a watch or something to tell the time."

"I have placed a two-centimeter-square silver plate on your left sleeve at your wrist. Just tap it, and the time will appear in a hologram above it."

"Look, it's twenty-two hundred. I think I will go take a shower and go to bed. Please beam me to my bedroom." Just like that, I was in my bedroom. "Thank you."

I took off my clothes and threw them on the floor. *Hmm*, I thought, *nowhere else to throw them*. I walked into the bathroom and then into the shower.

The shower was nice. From the top to the bottom, every ten centimeters in all four corners was a sprayer. It was really nice to have real water again. There was a knob on the wall to adjust the temperature, and it had a temperature readout above it. Above that was a silver plate about ten centimeters square to activate the soap spray from the neck down. I just had to lean over to get my head soapy. Then I would tap the square again to shut off the soap and rinse off. I tapped the knob to shut off the spray, and by the time I stepped out of the shower, I was dry; there was no need for a towel.

I walked out of the bathroom and looked around. My old clothes were gone, and just the bed was in the room.

"Athena, could we add underwear to my wardrobe? Boxer-briefs please."

Just like that, a pair of boxer-briefs was floating in the air in front of me. I took them and looked around again.

"Athena, would you please place a meter-square table against the forward wall with a chair so I can put my clothes on it?"

I put on my underwear and climbed into bed and fell asleep.

The next morning, when I woke up, the lights gently came on.

"Athena."

Just then a multipointed starlike object appeared, floating at the foot of my bed.

"What is that?"

"This is my new avatar." It reverberated as she spoke. *"What do you think?"*

"Okay, cool. What time is it? Wait; let's put a dial-face twelve-hour clock up. Make it part of the wall, with numbers, and make it illuminated ... about fifty centimeters in diameter on this wall—about halfway to the door on the dining room side—and about a hundred eighty centimeters from the floor." Just then the clock appeared on the wall. "Thank you. Oh, it's six o'clock."

I got out of bed and walked into the bathroom. Coming out, I saw that my clothes were on the table. I put them on. As I got up out of the chair, I said, "Athena, I think I'll make my breakfast this morning if you please."

As I walked into the kitchen, the lights came on.

"Athena, if you would please, I would like three jumbo eggs, a three-cup bowl, a knife and fork, two tablespoons of butter, three sausage patties, a thirty-centimeter skillet, and a sixteen-ounce cup of my coffee. Please heat the pan to one hundred ninety degrees Celsius."

I cooked up my breakfast, took it to the table, and sat down to eat. There was my glass of tomato juice, and right behind me was Athena's avatar, who came around and hovered at the other end of the table. As I was eating my breakfast, I said, "Athena, status report please."

"It's 0-six-thirty. All shields are holding and are at 50 percent. No sign of the radiation penetrating the shields. I have had to gradually adjust power to maintain a speed of 40 percent of light speed. We are twenty and a half hours from the barrier. All systems are normal."

I finished my breakfast, grabbed my coffee cup, got up and went to the living room, stood there, and started thinking. Athena's avatar came around and hovered in front of me.

"Athena, refill please. Thank you. We have a little over twenty hours to go, and you have plenty to do. I can sit here and watch a couple of movies, I guess."

After five hours, I had watched a couple of movies and listened to some music and had lunch.

"Athena, status report please."

"It's twelve hundred hours. All shields are holding and are at 75 percent. No sign of the radiation penetrating the shields. Damping and structure fields are good. Still adjusting engine power as predicted. We are fifteen hours from the barrier. All systems are operating as predicted."

I stepped up to the screen and asked Athena to show me the ships that were in tow, using the viewscreen. We spent the next two hours going over the structure we were using to tow the ships. It would have taken Athena a nanosecond to do this, but I did it to keep me busy. I spent another two hours examining the repairs we did on the First Ones' ships. Even with the repairs we did, they were far superior to the rest of the ships, but they were still not operating as they should have been.

I then sat down on the sofa and listened to some music and watched the pink nothing. After an hour and a half, I debated on supper and went to the dining room, where I sat down and had beef stew with a tall ice-cold glass of lager.

"Athena, status report please."

Athena's avatar replied, *"It's eighteen hundred hours, and all shields are holding and are at 100 percent. No sign of the radiation penetrating the shields. The damping and structure fields are good. I am still adjusting engine power as predicted. We are nine hours from the barrier. All systems are operating as predicted."*

"Athena, could you beam me down to you?" I was there in the blink of an eye. "Thank you." As I appeared, the hologram surrounded me. I looked around in all directions and said, "Athena, only we have come into this Nebula in the last three hundred fifty years, right?"

"Yes."

"Has it been this long between ships before?"

"In the last two thousand years, there has never been more than a fifty-year gap between ships. Why that is, is a very good question, and I cannot answer it. I've also been studying their star charts, and their timelines do not seem to line up. I'm still working on it. Once we get out of here and see the stars around us, I can figure it out."

I continued to look at the ships in tow and saw the screen flicker. Athena informed me, *"The radiation is starting to affect the scanners."*

I tapped my wrist to see the time. It was twenty hundred hours.

I said, "Athena, I think I will try to get some sleep. Beam me to my bedroom please."

Before I could finish speaking, I was standing in my bedroom. I took my clothes off and put them on the table and took a shower. I came out, and a clean pair of underwear was on the table. I put them on, and there was my tomato juice. I drank my juice and climbed into bed and said, "Athena, status report please."

Athena's avatar replied, *"It's twenty thirty hours, and all shields are holding and are at 125 percent. No sign of the radiation penetrating the shields. The shields, and damping and structure fields are fluctuating. I am still adjusting engine power as predicted. We are six and a half hours from the barrier. All systems are operating as predicted."*

I closed my eyes and fell asleep.

The lights came on, and Athena's avatar, at the foot of the bed, said, *"The shields and structure fields have failed. It's 0-one-thirty. We are an hour and a half from the barrier, and the scanners are fluctuating more often now."*

I put on my clothes, and Athena beamed me down to her. She had a table and a glass of tomato juice waiting for me. I drank the juice and stood there watching the ships in tow. After a while, the screen went blank.

"We have entered the barrier."

"So it begins," I said.

For the next hour and half, I watched the graph that Athena put up that showed the percentage of the radiation penetrating the hull. The radiation had started penetrating the hull five minutes after we entered the barrier. It was now at 50 percent.

"Athena, how far have we traveled? Can you tell?"

"My best estimation is two hundred seventy-five million kilometers. We have gone over our estimated thickness of the barrier. Should we return?"

"No," I said, "we will continue until the last possible minute."

"Once we lose the engines, you will have less than an hour before the radiation penetrates this room and kills you. I can give the engines enough power just before we lose them to get the ship out of the barrier and the radiation field. We will lose the tow structure, but this will be for your safety."

Another hour and twenty minutes went by before Athena announced, *"In another ten minutes, I will execute a turnaround and engine blast."*

"Don't use the word 'execute' now. Gee whiz. Just hold on."

The ten minutes went by.

"Executing ... Sorry. Starting turn."

"No, wait," I said. "Give me just one more minute."

"No sir. Starting turn. Wait; scanners are clearing. We are exiting the Nebula. The barrier has slowed us down immensely. Adjusting power. Stingray will be clear in four, three, two, one ... We are clear. The towed ships we be clear in ... the tow structure is badly damaged. Starting repairs. All ten ships are clear. Tow structure is repaired. We are picking up speed. Adjusting power. We are ten million kilometers and—"

It was as though the universe blinked.

"What was that? Did we lose power or something?"

"No. Systems check okay. Wait; I have lost three seconds. That's impossible. Checking. Yes, I lost three seconds. Checking all systems again. All systems check okay. All six towed ships are present."

"Let me see them. Okay, yeah, all six ships are okay. Turn on the scanners to full power. Let's see how good these scanners really are. We have never have gotten to test the new and improved ones after we modified them from the First Ones'. Hey, wait; where are their ships? Didn't they make it out of the nebula with us?"

"Checking. Yes they did." Athena played back the exit. *"See, they did make it out, but when we got to ten million kilometers, they disappeared, along with some of their memories that they were with us. But I still have all their data, I think. Wait a minute; the forest is gone."*

CHAPTER TEN

First Meeting

I studied the view and said, "Let's get some distance from this thing and figure this out."

Athena was quiet for a second and then said, *"There are three large clusters of ships around the Nebula. Each cluster has a station and a warning beacon."*

"Let's conceal ourself and get some distance away and find a place to hide for now, until we figure this out," I replied.

We found a spot that was blind to all three clusters. The scanners turned out to be a lot better than we had thought. We could scan in great detail at ten light years away and make something out at twenty-eight hundred light years. Athena started scanning everything and in less than ten minutes had scanned everything within in ten light years

"There is a time dilation between the outside of the Nebula and the inside," Athena said, *"but first the surrounding sector—the only ships in this sector are ones here or*

the ones traveling to one of these clusters; all other ships are avoiding this sector. The Nebula is moving along a course toward a giant white star. Stand by. Our star charts have been updated. I have the path of the Nebula. It came from outside of the galaxy. It has destroyed eight white stars, so the moons are what's left of the white stars it consumed. It does not stray far from its path, and its slow; it's averaging less than half the speed of light. Every time it encounters a system, it is slowed down, it does regain its speed, but the time that takes depends on how big the system is. It has taken over fifty-three thousand years to get here and has another four hundred years to go to get to the next white giant, which is almost two hundred light years away—if it is not slowed by these three systems that are in the way. It looks like the dragon-keeper's civilization came from that last system."

Athena changed the hologram from the Nebula path to all three of the clusters. She then continued with her analysis. *"There are three clusters, each with a large station and a warning beacon at the center, and none of them can see us. The three warning beacons are the same and are made by the First Ones. The station on the front right side is the most advanced, but I'm way more advanced than any of them. They are the most dedicated to the science of the Nebula. They also have on board most of the civilizations we are seeking, but there are a couple of the old ones that are not here or any records that they were. We have only one of their ships— that elegant tanker, and the six-thousand-meter cargo ship. I think we can leave the rest of the ships with them; they can get word back to the civilizations where the ships came from and can be picked up on their next trip to the station. The station on the left side of the Nebula is more like a trading post, and the one on the right is a military outpost. The warning beacons are broadcasting, "Do not enter nebula—kills all."*

Now the hologram changed to the tow structure.

"The First Ones did an excellent job on it," Athena said. "I cannot tell where they removed the part of the structure we tethered their ship to. All the builder drones are accounted for, and the excess material from the tow structure was put in the cargo

ships I was using in the cargo hold of Stingray. I still can't believe they wanted our forest."

"Well, it was a good trade for the updated star charts and for all the technology, don't you think?"

"When you think of it that way, yes, it was a very good trade."

I was looking at the hologram of the center station, and I asked, "Athena, could you scan that station without them knowing about it?"

"Yes, I can scan all three of the stations without them knowing it. This one was built by linguists and the scanner ship's civilization, and their systems haven't changed that much. This is easy. What do you wish to know?"

"I would like to know if they know anything of the First Ones?"

"Just the old story of an old race that protects this region of space, and this is one of its warning beacons."

The hologram was now focused on the center station and the warning beacon. The beacon was a Truncated Cuboctahedron. It had twelve square faces, eight regular hexagonal faces, six regular octagonal faces, forty-eight vertices, and seventy-two edges and was flashing red, and the station was the size and shape of my previous station but had docking pods.

"Athena, can we communicate with that station to let them know what we want to do without scaring them?"

"Yes. Communicating with them now. I let them know the time and place where we came out of the nebula. They are asking what happened to the people in the ships. I let them know no one survived entering the nebula. They said they will be more than happy to take the ships—especially the dragon-keeper's ship. They would be honored."

We made our way to the station, keeping the belly side of the ship out of the sight of their scanners. Even though they could not see *Stingray* on their scanner at all, Athena gave them something of a false image on their scanners, making them think they could. When we arrived, I had Athena start materializing the ships on the underside so they would be out of sight of the station. They might start asking too many questions about the technology of this ship and Athena's capabilities if the ships just started to appear. Athena made sure that all the ships that were going to the station were restored to their original configuration, and all data that mentioned the First Ones, the advanced technology that Athena had discovered, and God's Metal were deleted, because it appeared that the First Ones didn't want others to know too much about them. And I didn't want them to know too much about Athena.

The ships that Athena had scan the station computer couldn't handle all the details, so Athena gave them the most that they could handle. Athena beamed the ships that were in the transporter buffer and the cargo bay underneath *Stingray*. The ones that weren't going to the station. The six-thousand-meter cargo ship, the replicator ship, the mining ship, and the tanker were still in the tow structure. She also kept all the cargo. Athena had the builder drones tow the ships to a staging area.

It turned out that there were 424 ships; we had thought the oldest one of these entered the Nebula two thousand years ago, but Athena checked the archive records of the station and found out it had disappeared three thousand years ago. We learned there was a time dilation; the longer one was in the nebula, the greater the difference in time. So the time the last ship entered the nebula wasn't two hundred years ago but more like three hundred years. The First Ones' ships entered the Nebula, according to Athena's new calculations, over forty-nine thousand years ago. So the First

Ones were now more advanced than we first thought—a lot more advanced. That's probably how they were able to do what they did when they retrieved their ships, and how they were able to stop the other races from fighting or interfering with each other.

"I wonder if they can travel through time, because they did a lot of work in that three seconds," Athena said. *"They may have taken those three seconds to let us know they were there, to see what we would do. Also that's why they could retrieve the ships so fast—they had all the time they needed to come back and get their ships when and where they wanted. The other thing is that they let us keep all the technology and did not try too hard at taking all our memories about their ships. Stand by."*

"I have monitored a message sent to that military outpost. It says, 'A big ship has emerged from the nebula with one of your ships; you need to come quick.' They are dispatching a large warship a little bigger than the one we found in the Nebula. It will be here in about an hour. Should I stop it?"

"No, let it come," I replied. "We don't want to give away too much insight to your capabilities. Let's see what they will do, but if they start to fire, you can stop them."

"The station is calling and asking how we were able to survive and the others weren't."

"Tell them our hull slowed the radiation enough to let us get in and then out with the ships. I don't want them to know that we built *Stingray* in the Nebula or that we were in there for over a hundred years and found all these civilizations, since some of the old ones are not even represented here."

"Stand by. The warship is demanding we turn over all prisoners and data or they will open fire on us."

"Tell them we have no prisoners and that's all the data they are getting, period."

Athena relayed the message; the warship moved in closer. Athena turned *Stingray* and came head-to-head with the warship. The warship was a little over thirty-five hundred meters long, while *Stingray* was over thirty-seven thousand meters long—ten times bigger than it. Being so close, the warship could see the difference in size. Athena dropped the false image, and the captain of the warship grew a little worried, as the only way to see *Stingray* was visually. They no longer had a weapons lock, and *Stingray* filled the viewscreen. After a second or two, the warship turned away and headed to the station.

Athena reported, *"The warship relayed a message back to the outpost to send for the fleet. They replied that it would be a couple of months before they could get here and asked what if it's 'them.' The warship replied that it was not 'them' but one of the other races that built a giant cargo ship, because they saw no weapons. Well, he is sort of right. What should we do?"*

"Nothing. How about going to the Dragon-Keeper system to see what happened."

*"I think I should take the Dragon-Keepers' ship back; it's up for auction at the trading post. They plan on stealing it from the Grammatica race, and I don't think they have a choice in the matter."[1]**

"Can you do it without them noticing it?"

"Yes I can. I can make it look like a false echo until they run a detailed scan, which they haven't done yet."

"Do it."

"Done. I replaced it with another that looks like it but is a piece of junk on the inside. They will never notice it isn't the real one; they will think we made a mistake."

"Athena, bring up the star chart of this region and locate the system,"

---

[1] * *"Grammatica"* is Latin for "linguistics."

"The system is twelve hundred fifty light years from here; how fast do you want to get there? Remember: we have the tow structure and four ships in it."

"Why don't we see if we can get *Stingray* up to warp ten with them. Do it slowly; I don't want to break the ship the first time out, especially here. That would be embarrassing."

Athena started reading off the warp scale. *"Warp one, warp two, warp three …"* She went all the way to warp ten. *"All systems normal, no unusual vibration, nice and smooth. The engine is running at 35 percent."*

"We are going what, a thousand times the speed of light and as smooth as silk at only 35 percent, towing four ships. Wow. I knew I would keep saying that. How long will it take for us to get there?"

Athena replied, *"At this speed, with these ships and this tow structure, about four hundred fifty-six days, what should we do now?"*

"I don't know; can we increase speed at all?"

"I'll see what I can do."

"I don't know about you," I said, "but I'm hungry. I would like to go up to the dining room and have a steak dinner and a lager."

Just like that, I was in my dining room. On the table was a salad, a steak with a baked potato and green beans, and a tall, ice-cold glass stein of lager.

After dinner, I said, "Athena, would you please refill my stein and turn on the screen to forward view."

As I stood there watching, a big grin came across my face.

"Athena, we made it out, and here we are, among the stars, doing warp ten. Wow."

Athena's avatar floated over to my side and said, *"It is something. How do you feel? It's 0-one-hundred; you have been up for twenty-four hours."*

"I feel fine, but I am a little tired. I think I will go to bed now after a shower." After I took my shower, I climbed into bed and asked,

"Athena, could you project the forward view at the foot of my bed?" The hologram appeared. "Thank you, that is so cool. Good night, Athena."

"Good night."

The next day, Athena was able to reconfigure the tow structure to hold just the four ships and learn how to tune the shields and was able to get us up to warp fourteen. Now the trip would take only 166 days. We had to get rid of the tow structure, so we started studying the star charts.

It had been thirty-eight days since we started our journey to the Dragon-Keeper system, and we had been studying the star charts we gathered at the stations and the updates the First Ones gave us, and we had also been scanning systems along the way. There was a lot of data to look over, and those thirty-eight days went by fast.

Athena found a system that she thought she could mine for the resources she needed. Most of the civilizations at the stations did not know of it yet because it was 856 lightyears from them, and very few of them could do more than warp ten. The best of them could do warp fifteen, and that was only with their fast attack ships, and there were very few of them.

I spent the next twenty-one days going over some more new science that Athena had learned in these past hundred years.

After dinner, I sat in front of the viewscreen, thinking of what to do. "Athena, how's that system with the giant asteroid belts looking?"

"I don't have a detail scan of the system yet, but it is looking very good and will be more than enough to top off everything I need. We will be there in fifty-three days."

"Okay," I replied. "Is there any chance on getting any more speed out of *Stingray?* I know towing these ships is slowing us down, but can we tune the shields any more? I know you have been learning new techniques for warp speed ever since we started doing warp speed."

"I have, and I can fine-tune the shields. I'm learning a lot about the effects of the shield harmonics and warp speed. I can also bring up the structure fields on the tow structure to 110 percent. We should be able to get to warp eighteen and cut our travel time down to twenty-six days."

"That's a whole lot better. Can you do it while we are in warp, or do we have to stop?"

"Please. Adjusting shields now ... warp fifteen ... warp sixteen ... warp seventeen ... warp eighteen. The fields are holding. No abnormal strain on the tow structure."

"At this system we are going to, do you think we can get enough material to build that biosphere? That apartment is a little confining."

"Oh, definitely. I can turn the whole cargo bay into a biosphere if you want."

"No, just the top of the computer room will do. Twelve hundred fifty acres is good enough. Well, I think I'll go take a shower and head to bed."

After my shower, I crawled into bed and had Athena bring up the hologram of the forward view.

"This I'll never get tired of. Good night, Athena."

"Good night."

CHAPTER ELEVEN

My New Home

I woke up, and the star field hologram was still on at the foot of the bed. Athena's avatar was at the right side of the bed, close to the foot of it. "This is so cool. Good morning, Athena. How are you?"

Athena's avatar turned on the lights just a little and replied, *"I feel great. Stingray is operating perfectly. No abnormalizes to report. How are you?"*

"I feel great, thanks. How about some bacon—six strips—two eggs over easy, two slices of toast with butter, a mug of my coffee, a glass of tomato juice, and … let's see … oh, a peeled orange."

That morning we arrived at the system Athena wanted to mine for resources. For the past twenty-six days, I had been kept very busy with Athena's new science. Thanks to that learning part of the suspended animation, things had not been difficult.

By the time I finished dressing, I could smell my breakfast, so I quickly stepped into the dining room, sat down at the table, and said,

"That smells great! Thanks, Athena. While I'm eating, we should go over the design of the biosphere. How tall should we make it?"

"How big of trees do you want? I can make some Redwoods if you'd like."

"Yes, have the dome a hundred meters high, and have four redwoods about seventy meters tall in the middle, with a large creek running diagonal from the southwest to the northeast, going around the southeast side of the of the four redwoods. On the northwest side, have fruit and nut trees with berry bushes along the walls and a garden about an acre in size, and in the southern sector, have citrus trees, and along the wall have grape and vegetables vines. On the northeast side, have a ten-acre pond, not too close to the wall, with its southern border a sandy beach, and then have the citrus trees in the southeast corner and have bridges over the creek. We can figure out where later. The rest of the wall space should have flowers. And make the northwest corner a sixteen-acre pasture. What else? Oh yeah, make sure there is plenty of room for your sphere to get around the trees and bushes."

"How about an observation deck at the top of the dome? I can make it with glass walls and a raised platform so you can see the cargo hold too."

"That sounds good. Make it big enough for your sphere to be in. Maybe we will make it into the bridge. Do you have enough material to do it?" I looked at the hologram of it in my living room.

Athena said, *"Yes, this system we just entered has a couple of asteroid belts that I can mine. It will be enough to supply us for a several years. It will take just two days to get the material we need."*

"Does it belong to anyone, or is there any warning buoy?, We are going to have to keep an eye out, or do you have their location marked on the star charts.

"There are no signs of anyone claiming this sector, and I have most of the locations for the warning buoys on the star charts, but they can always put more out there. We are approaching the outer asteroid belt."

"Okay, beam me down next to you."

Athena slowed the ship, and we entered the asteroid belt. "The Nebula came through here and destroyed the star that was here, which destroyed all the planets. Scanning. I don't see any evidence that anyone was here. There are a lot of base elements here. Would you like any gold?"

"Oh yeah. How much?"

"How many metric tons would you like? One million or two?"

"Million or two? Huh, maybe, we'll see. Any other unique elements in this system?"

"To us, yes. Here, not really. Oh wait; there are two elements I can get. I can make a base out of one and a sphere out of the other, causing the sphere to levitate. How about that?"

"Great. Can we make a ten-meter sphere? Do the First Ones have a name for this system?"

"Yes, but when I translate it, it doesn't make any sense. But 'Natantes Crystallini' in Latin means 'floating diamonds.' I found one, and it's roughly a hundred quintillion carats."

"Okay, what, a hundred-quintillion-carat diamond, where, oh,. Wow. I don't think that will fit in the ship."

"Actually, there are a couple of others, though not as big—only a couple quadrillion carats—there at the center of the system. Must be what's left of the star's core."

"Wow," I said. "Must have broken apart somehow. Now they sit there and slowly spin. Hey, are they causing the asteroids to orbit?"

"At this point, I don't know if the big asteroids in the innermost belt are creating the gravity field or if it's the diamonds—or both. I will need some time to study this."

"Okay, 'Natantes Crystallini' is Latin for 'floating diamonds'; what is Latin for 'spinning Diamonds?'"

"Latin for 'spinning diamonds' is 'spheara crystallini.'"

"Spheara crystallini. I hope we get better at naming planets and civilizations later on. Okay, engrave the name on the sphere. Anything else? Oh, wait; could I have lunch here? Just one of your hoagies and some … hmm, let's try some iced tea." A table appears with the hoagie and iced tea on it. "Thank you. I want to watch you do some mining. I know that sounds a little boring, but I want to see how you do it. And by the way, where are you going to put the material?"

"Yes, there are other things, but nothing real interesting, I will place some of it in the pit. I will make five-hundred-square-meter cubes that hold about 125 million cubic meters, about fifty-five of them, and place them in there. In the alcoves alongside the cargo hold side wall, I will make one-thousand-square-meter cubes that hold about one billion cubic meters—but only eight of them on each side. Here is a list of all the material we are mining." Athena placed a list on the hologram.

"There is a lot."

It was really neat to watch the builder-drones take apart the asteroids and remove the materials we wanted. Some of the asteroids had liquid metal in them, and splitting them to get it out looked like we were cracking open an egg. There were also a lot more diamonds floating around. So we went ahead and cut a diamond. It was a billion carats after it was cut, and we placed it in the basement with the sphere. The diamond was an Asscher-cut clear diamond about the size of a car.

Athena beamed me back to the dining room to have supper.

After supper, Athena informed me, *"The biosphere is finished; would you like to see it?"*

"Yes, place me in the observation deck please." I was there in the blink of an eye. "Thank you. This is cool. Maybe we should get rid of the glass in the walls from the observation deck to the biosphere. We have this railing, and if I do fall out, you can always catch me."

"Hmm."

Just then I felt something change about my clothing. "What was that? Did you just change my clothes?" I said.

"Sort of. I added an antigravity webbing in your clothes. Now if you fall out, you will just float. Go ahead; give it a try." She removed the glass and a section of the railing.

I looked over the side and down at the forest floor. "A hundred meters is a long way down; I don't think—" Just then I felt a push, and out I went.

I was just floating there outside the observation deck, upside-down, looking at the forest. I looked back at Athena and righted myself.

"Did you just push me out the window?" I asked.

"Yes. I said I would always give you a nudge in the right direction."

"Ha ha."

I looked down at my left hand and saw the familiar EV thruster pack controls. I lowered myself to the forest floor. A flash went by me, and then I was standing in the southwest corner, next to the creek, looking around.

I was about to call up to Athena, but she was in front of me. "Oh, you took the easy way down."

"I beat you down."

"Oh, the flash that went by me." I kept looking around, thinking. "Athena, could you mine some plain dirt and rocks, and, let's see, put a two-acre pond and three acres of land at the southwest corner wall and raise it about twelve meters high with a three-tiered waterfall, with each tier's pond about sixteen meters square? Have the upper pond about one and half meters deep and the others a meter deep each. Gradually bring it down to this level. And make the water twenty-six degrees Celsius in the top pond; I want to be able to swim in it. And make the air temperature about twenty degrees Celsius."

"Yes, but you will have to stand over here by me." Athena herself was hovering in a small clearing just big enough for her sphere.

"Okay, where are you? Oh, there you are; give me a minute." I ran over by her, about ten meters from where I had been. "It's a good thing you spread the trees out. Okay, do it." The ground rose, and the pond and the waterfalls formed. "This is so cool. Hmm, I don't think that is gradual enough. Maybe you should double it."

"Okay, but we will have to move over there." she started moving, brushing the trees along the way over to an area she had indicated with her avatar about forty meters away.

I ran alongside her to the spot. "How about that, I can run again. Maybe I will ask you to put in a jogging path for me. Okay, go ahead and do it." The hill and the waterfall stretched out. "That looks great. Now let's go up there and see how that looks." I ran up to the top of the hill as Athena floated alongside me. We got to the top, and I started looking around. "Okay, see these five trees that border this clearing? Please transplant them to the edge of the pasture. Now let's put an apartment here, about twelve meters by twelve meters, with four rooms—a bathroom, a living room, an eat-in kitchen, and a bedroom—with no outside walls except the bathroom, with the bathroom and bedroom on the north side. And have the living room close enough to the south wall to have a big deck going to the wall so I can walk out onto it and see out the glass to the cargo bay. Oh, have the apartment above the ground so I just need to take a step up into it."

"Okay, just step back two meters ... There, how's that?"

"That's great." I stepped into the bedroom and looked out into the biosphere and up to the dome. "Not as high as I thought. Can you make this level about forty meters above ground level, but not too close to the dome."

"Sure, hold on."

The apartment and the surrounding area around started to rise. Now I could see most of the biosphere from here; it was like looking down over a valley. Athena had to raise the dome only about ten meters in this corner.

"Athena, look at the time, it's O-one hundred. We should dim the lights down in the bay and put the lights on a twenty-four-hour cycle." The lights dimmed to twilight in the biosphere. I walked over to the deck and looked out into the bay. "You can see the whole bay, and with the lights dimmed, you can just make out the outline of the bay. Impressive job, Athena. That looks great."

I turned around, walked through the living room into the kitchen, and grabbed my glass of tomato juice. Then I walked back outside and looked at Athena hovering close to ground in front of me and said, "Athena I wouldn't be able to do these twenty thousand years without you. I hope you are planning on sticking around. And thank you for making this possible." Then I looked straight up and said, "And thank you, God, for Athena."

I swear I heard Athena say, "Amen."

"Well it's time for bed, Athena. How's the mining going?"

"I should be done in about thirty-eight hours. Would you like any more diamonds or gems? I have found a large deposit of all kinds of gems."

"So what happened here?" I asked

"When the Nebula came through here, it caused the star to somewhat implode, causing a gravity well that drew in all the planets, and after a while they started to collide with each other, breaking apart. The asteroid belt is still forming. The gravity well that was causing them to draw to the center of the system has burned itself out and no longer exists. That big diamond is part of a sun's core. According to the star charts, there were eight large planets that were rich in materials and uninhabited by life forms of any kind. All but two of the outer planets had atmospheres—nothing breathable for you, though."

"About the gems, I'll let you know in the morning. I'm going to take a shower and go to bed."

I walked into the bathroom and noticed what I thought was a window that stretched along the outside walls but didn't have any glass. There was a mirror above the sink. After my shower, I went to bed. Athena turned down the house lights and placed the hologram view at the foot of the bed, and I fell asleep.

I woke up when I felt a gentle breeze and noticed Athena was in the same place she had been in when I fell asleep. Athena brought up the lights, and I said, "Good morning, Athena; you still here?"

"Yes, I can run everything from wherever I'm at. I thought you might want to go over a few things, like the schedule of the lighting in the biosphere. It's 0-eight hundred; I'll be finished mining in thirty-two hours."

I looked at the hologram, smiled, got out of bed, and went into the bathroom.

"Okay," I said, coming out of the bathroom. I started putting on my clothes. "The lights. Okay, at night have the light as bright as a clear starlit night on Earth, and at about O-five hundred, start bringing them up. By O-eight hundred, have the lights during the day on about as bright as a somewhat cloudy day. Then, at twenty hundred, start bringing them down to starlight, which they should reach by twenty-two hundred." I got up out of the chair, walked over to Athena, and looked out over the biosphere and saw movement. "I see you have maintenance drones working already. Can I have one get me a couple oranges and lemons?"

"Is there anything else you would like for breakfast?"

"Yes, three scrambled eggs and six strips of bacon, coffee, and instead of tomato juice, could I get a glass of milk, please." I sat down at the table, and there was my breakfast and a large crystal bowl. "Nice bowl. For the fruit, I presume?"

Just then a drone came gliding in and deposited the fruit. I heard a noise in the living room and saw two more drones placing apples and nuts into their own large crystal bowls on the coffee table. I finished my breakfast and grabbed an orange, peeled and ate it, and then grabbed a lemon and did the same. "Man, those were good; you are getting a pretty good green thumb there, Athena."

"I have no thumbs."

I put my hand over my face and said, "Oh no," and started laughing. I sat straight up. "The gems. Okay, let's see; do you have any platinum?"

"Oh yes."

"Okay, how about making a platinum pedestal a meter high, in the shape of an emerald cut, with the base about seventy-five centimeters square and the top about fifty centimeters square. On top of the pedestal, make a bowl made from five emerald-cut sapphires about fifty centimeters square, held together with silver settings. And fill the bowl with hundred-carat gems. Okay?" It appeared after a few seconds. "Wow, that is something. Nice touch with the light. How much do you have?"

"I filled a one-thousand-square- meter container."

"That's a billion cubic meters of gemstones. That's a lot; why so much? I'm not really complaining, just wondering."

"At the trading post station, most of the civilizations used real gemstone for trading."

"So we're rich?" I asked

"No, we are stinking rich. The artwork we just made could buy a starship."

"So these are not replicated?" I asked. "Oh, that's why it took a few second to make."

"No, they are not replicated. I had to cut them first and then transport them here. And one more thing—it's ten hundred hours."

"Okay, what happens at ten hundred hours?" Just then it started to rain.

"I make it rain at ten hundred and sixteen hundred."

"Oh, okay. How about at bedtime too." I said as I walked closer to Athena, who had a shield she was using as an umbrella, "Smells nice. I like this."

I looked up at Athena, and just as I was about to say something else, she stated, *"I don't rust."*

I started laughing and said, "Okay, let's go to the computer room." Just like that, we were there. "Okay, bring up the asteroid field and see how things are going."

"I have found that the innermost asteroids' orbit has become stable and is causing the rest of the asteroids in the belt to become stable as well, and it does look like the big diamonds started it. There is a very large asteroid in a stable orbit around the center of this system; it's almost fifteen hundred kilometers by two thousand kilometers and

appears to be ideal to build a complex in to house the probes and the other ships. It has a very large cavern with a narrower opening we can use as a hangar bay, and we can build structures in the other caverns coming off the main one, like labs, warehouses, and living quarters—you know, just in case."

"Can *Stingray* fit in it? If so, we can use it as a base."

"I just have to remove a couple of boulders and Stingray can easily fit through. It will take only a day to build it. We can also setup a monitoring lab to watch the system reform itself."

"Okay, sure, why not? It would be nice to have a place on this side of the galaxy."

So Athena got some more builder drones out and started building the complex, and I had lunch. The drones were busy, and I was watching everything on the holograph. Then I saw the ships being towed into the asteroid.

"Athena, can we beam the elegant tanker into the cargo hold? We should try to find the owners."

"Okay, stand by. Wait, this is proving to be difficult. There. That took some doing. It was as if there was more than what was there. I have checked to ensure the tanker is empty. It was as though I were transporting several of the huge cargo ships. Now we have two ships in the cargo hold: the tanker and the Dragon-Keepers'. Even though the tanker is smaller, it was more difficult to transport then the Dragon-Keepers' ship."

I continued to watch the mining operation until suppertime. After supper Athena and I went up to the observation deck, and she brought up the hologram of the mining operation and the building of the complex again, and I watched it until ten o'clock that night, eating fruit from the biosphere.

The following morning after breakfast, Athena informed me the complex was finished.

"So you finished it. Can we go over to look around?"

"Yes." We were there in the blink of an eye. *"What do you think?"*

"Wow, this is straight out of a science fiction movie," I said excitedly.

We were in an observation room looking out into the hangar bay with *Stingray* just coming into the bay, and *Stingray* just fit through the opening but glided through it as though it were nothing. Even with the ships and the probes, there was still plenty of room for *Stingray* to maneuver around.

We turned around and headed into the reception area. Right in the middle of the room, on a big platinum stand, was a big emerald-cut diamond that looked to be about ten billion carats. This thing was huge.

"Couldn't help yourself, huh," I said, chuckling a little.

"What do you mean? It's a decoration; it brightens up the room."

"Yeah, sure it does."

"I have a park down that hallway."

Some hallway it was. It was at least thirty meters wide and three stories tall, with two levels of decks looking over it. The park was at least ten acres, it was in the center of this cavern with the ceiling fifty meters above us.

"Nicely done, Athena. What are these hotel-like rooms?"

"Certainly not, apartments—single to four bedrooms, all first class and up. The owner's penthouse is up there."

"Wow, is that what that is."

"The mining is complete, Stingray is restocked, and I filled the warehouses in the complex. I'm going to leave about ten builder drones here. The computer system I'm leaving should be able to handle the job of running this place."

"Well, I've seen enough for now. So we have what we need?"

"Yes, everything is aboard Stingray, and we are ready to depart. The tow structure is dismantled."

"Good. How about we get underway. We can come back later for shore leave."

CHAPTER TWELVE

The Journey Begins

With the mining complete, we arrived at the Dragon-Keepers' system seventeen days later. For the past couple of weeks, I had been keeping myself busy with all the data from the Dragon-Keepers' ship. It took Athena just minutes, me, I'm a little slower.

The data informed us that this system had a giant white star and six planets, with the Dragon Keepers having come from the second planet. Their ship was the last ship to leave and had been hurriedly put together because they were the ones that had not believed it would happen and waited too long. The ship had just cleared the atmosphere when it was swallowed up. How the ship made it through the barrier but the planets didn't was another mystery, mainly because there was nothing left of the planets bigger than a molecule.

Since this was the last ship to leave, it just had the basic library with no current data on where the rest of the race went to. The last ones didn't brother to load the current data; they didn't think they needed to, because they thought everyone would be back after it went past. Once they saw the outer planet being destroyed, they hurriedly got the ship ready, but they were too late.

We came out of warp at the edge of where the system should have been and entered a massive dust cloud. There was nothing left of this system.

"Scanning. Nothing but dust. There are no signs of a civilization ever being here. The only way to mine this system is with a scoop. There is a mystery here: why can ship go through the barrier while planets are totally destroyed? In the last system we mined, the Nebula came in just above the elliptical orbit of the planets, skimming the sun outer corona but not touching the planets."

"I think we should leave their ship here as a monument to the race that lived here. We have copied all data. Maybe one day the First Ones will put a warning beacon here."

"Transporting the ship ... The ship is transported. Oh my, there is a warning beacon at the bow of the ship. I didn't put it there, and I saw nothing."

"Does it say anything?"

"'You may come and learn of the Dragon-Keepers; knowledge is all you can remove.'"

"Okay, that's it. Have you got all the scans you need? Athena, I just had a thought. What if the people leaving the buoys is us? What if, in the future, you are able to master time travel and do this? Wait a minute; why would we take the forest?"

"It could be both the First Ones and us. Where do you want to go next?"

"That's a thought. Do you know where the memory cores' shell came from?"

"Yes. It's about nine hundred seventy-eight light years from here. It will take forty-four point five days at warp twenty to get there."

"Any systems along the way that seem interesting?" I asked.

"Yes. Three. And there's another with a warning beacon, this one saying not to interfere. We can be at the first system in eleven days."

"Okay. Did we disturb the dust much when we came in?"

"Yes, but we can go back over it and remove most of our trail signature so it will not be very noticeable. It will take several hours to get out of the system."

"That's okay," I replied. "It's not like we have very little time to do anything in."

As we cleared the system, we entered warp and left the system behind us. I noticed it was close to suppertime. *Darn, I forgot lunch; no wonder I'm hungry*, I thought. "Athena, can you beam me up to the kitchen? I think I'll have supper now." I was there in the blink of an eye. "Thank you." I looked outside. Athena had beamed up with me. I finished supper and walked out onto the deck to look out into the bay. I was now looking at the only ship we had left in the bay—the elegant tanker. I turned to look for Athena and saw that she was at the edge of the deck.

"Are you interested in the ship?"

"Yes, I am. Have you been able to translate anything yet?" I asked.

"Yes, I have made some progress since the last warning beacon. I have learned a couple of things about translating. By the way, new text has been added to the beacon's message. It says, 'Approach with respect.' It helped me in a way by using this tanker's language for some translating examples, and I think I should be able to translate the language in a few hours."

"Great, we can start exploring the ship tomorrow." I heard the waterfalls and smiled. "But for now, I think I will go swimming."

I walked into the bedroom and started to take off my clothes and looked around for a place to lay my clothes. I was going to lay them on the table, but Athena provided me with a valet stand, I put my clothes on the stand and was getting ready to walk out when the clothes disappeared and reappeared, I guess cleaned. I walked outside and over to the upper pond.

"Impressive job on the grass, Athena." I rubbed my feet through the grass and then jumped into the pond. "And the water is great." I swam over to the waterfall's edge and looked down at the next tier and started wondering. "Athena, how about a slide from this pond down along there to the next." I pointed from the middle of this pond down along the side of the waterfall to about the middle of the next tier.

"A slide? Okay, how's that. I suggest you put these on."

A pair of swimming trunks appeared at the edge of the slide, and I put them on. I climbed onto the slide and said, "Here I go ... Yeehaw! That was fun." I walked over to the falls and got under them. "This is nice. You have any soap that won't pollute the water?"

"Of course I do; it's on a shelf behind the falls."

"Thanks." I washed off and walked over to the edge of this tier of falls and looked out at the little valley. "Impressive job, Athena. This is really nice—better than being cooped up in *Aegis* for the rest of our lives. Could you have grown as much in *Aegis*?"

"There is no way of telling. There are too many factors, but I think I could not have grown anywhere near as much as I have here."

"Yeah, the Nebula was a good thing for us but terrible for all the others, so I guess we should learn as much as we can for them. Ah, twilight—it's getting late. I think I'll go inside."

I walked over to the bedroom. Just before going in, I took off my trunks and threw them into the air, and they disappeared. I had dried off by the time I got to the bedroom with a towel Athena materialized for me. It was hanging in midair, and I did the same with the towel as I did with the trunks. I walked into the bedroom and put on my shorts and noticed a pair of trunks and a towel clean and dry on the table. I walked into the living room, sat in the chair, and asked Athena, "Would you please bring up the star chart and show the path of the Nebula?"

"Of course. Here is the path of the Nebula, and here is our path and the stations, and this is where we are going."

The chart showed where the Nebula entered the galaxy and its path. It was somewhat like a crooked reentry trajectory headed for the center of the galaxy. Our path to our new destination was on the inside of the Nebula's path at an angle headed outward, toward the rim of the galaxy.

"The Nebula, as it consumes the giant white stars, is slowed down a lot by the process but picks up a little speed afterward. Since it has entered the galaxy, it has consumed eight stars and traveled about forty-eight hundred light years in the last fifty-three thousand years. It is averaging about .45 warp, or about half the speed of light. Here are the locations of the eight stars. There is another white star about one hundred sixty light years closer than the next star it's headed to but would require too much of a turn for it to make. Plus it's not as big."

"Do you have the location of the liquid memory planet and where the First Ones' ships entered the Nebula?" I asked. "The planet's system is on the rim of the galaxy, and the ships were swallowed up before the first star was consumed. Was the liquid memory planet's system destroyed by the Nebula?"

"It may have been. I do not detect any stars there. It's supposed to be a binary star system, but it is too far for a detailed scan."

"Well, that's okay; we won't be there for a couple of months anyway. So let's move to the planets we're going to be at in a couple of days. What are they like?"

"The star is an orange giant, with three gas giants, and they all have a lot of moons. The first gas giant is about 10.05 AU from the star and about six times the size of Jupiter. This giant has a radius of four hundred nineteen thousand kilometers and has twelve moons. The fifth and sixth moons have atmospheres and appear to have plant life. We will know more once we get there."

"That's good enough for now. I'm going to bed. Good night, Athena."

I walked into the bedroom and crawled into bed, and just then the rain started. I looked out and saw Athena hovering in the rain with no shield for an umbrella. I was going to say something, but I fell asleep.

The following morning, I woke up and Athena was still hovering in the same place. *Hmm, I think she might like it here.* "Good morning, Athena," I said. "Athena, do you sleep?"

"Not really. I sort of meditate. Stingray is somewhat autonomous; I just tell Stingray where to go and how fast, and I just monitor the results. I am capable of doing billions of functions a second, but while I'm meditating, that's cut in half."

"So you can do more in your sleep than I can while I'm awake," I said as I walked over to her.

"Yes, that's because I'm just a tad bit bigger than you are."

I looked up at her and said, "Just a tad bit bigger ... yeah, just a tad bit." I stood on my tiptoes with my hand over my head, trying to gauge her height, laughing a little as I went to get ready for breakfast.

After breakfast, I walked over to Athena and said, "I'm ready. You can activate my suit and beam me over to the tanker."

I appeared on the bridge of the tanker with Athena's avatar, and we started looking around. There were no chairs at the station, but it was loaded with control devices both on the panel and the floor, I accidently activated one, and something like a formula appeared just above eye level.

"Was that their language?"

"*Yes.*"

"What did they look like?"

Athena's avatar morphed into a representation, and I had to take a step back. What appeared was … well, the best way to describe it would be to say that it looked like a squid's body. It stood about two meters tall with ten tentacles about a meter long each at the base of the body, and midway up was another set of ten tentacles, also a meter long each. Halfway up from the upper tentacles were three eyes. The body was as thick as mine, and the eyes were spaced far enough apart that it had a 270-degree view. The body was covered, except for the two flaps at the top of the head, with an exoskeleton, along with half of each tentacle. Athena informed me that they breathed and heard through those flaps. They were like small elephant ears but had no holes; they felt vibrations. They had no mouth that I could see and didn't talk to each other but were telepathic. They fed themselves a sweet liquid of some kind through one of the upper tentacles. They were all one color—blue.

I walked down the halls with Athena's morphed avatar beside me—if you can call it walking. At the end of the exoskeleton on the lower tentacles were pads that it walked on.

Athena informed me that their language used various formulas that were for various types of science, such as navigation, engineering, biology, and so on. So she had to translate each science, and that took a while, especially because they used different symbols in each science. The creatures would communicate with these formulas telepathically to each other.

We walked down the hall to one of the tanks and came to a door. It was like all the other doors, so Athena opened it and I looked in. There was nothing inside but a big empty tank, but the door was just like all the others we had walked through.

"Athena, what did they store in here?"

"Nothing. I have scanned this tank serval times. Stand by. I found a microfracture that wasn't here before." Athena's morphed avatar floated over to the spot and pointed to it. *"This is not possible. I can see the other side, and it's a room the size of our computer room, and there are bodies— thousands of bodies. Wait; they're in suspended animation. They are alive."*

"Quick, stop the ship and beam me back to you and this ship outside," I said. I blinked and found myself standing next to Athena with *Stingray* stopped. The tanker was out in space. It took a few minutes, but the tanker took off. It went from zero to warp twenty-five in a split second. "That thing is fast; can you track it?"

"For now. Should we follow it?"

"I would like to, but I don't think we should."

"I left the morphed avatar on board with a visual record of what has happened and a way they can contact us if they want to. They can mind meld with it or scan it to learn everything."

"Let's get back underway and see what else we can learn today. By the way, did you learn how they were able to do those rooms and how many there were?"

"Not really, but I was able to copy their other database. To translate it may take a while. I could scan only that one tank, but after transporting the ship into space, two other tanks developed microfractures, and I was able to scan the other side. I think transporting them caused the microfractures. My scanner couldn't see anything through the fourth tank. In the two tanks were five thousand life forms each; the third held equipment. All three had a computer core that I could scan. I'm glad it took the ship a few minutes to come to life; it gave me time to scan the cores. There is a lot of information here."

"That should keep us busy for the next ten days while we make our way to our next stop."

We spent the next ten days studying the database. By the end of that time, we were coming close to deciphering the language, but we had to learn new sciences that we knew the First Ones didn't have at the time of the cargo ship entering the Nebula. In some ways, they were more advanced at that time, but they entered the Nebula thousands of years after the First Ones' ship did.

We came out of warp at the edge of the system and started scanning. The outer two gas giants were about twice the size of Jupiter. The outermost gas giant had fourteen moons, none with an atmosphere. The second gas giant had only six moons, and none of them had an atmosphere either. The inner gas giant was six times the size of Jupiter and had a radius of about four hundred nineteen thousand kilometers and has twelve moons, two of which—the fifth and sixth—had atmospheres.

"The fifth moon appears to be about the size of Earth and has trees and grasslands," Athena said. *"There is no sign of animal or insect life, and I don't think there will ever be unless something is introduced. The air is not breathable for you; there are a couple of elements that would not agree with you. Your suit is more than adequate to handle it. There is one more thing this atmosphere is good for; and that is flying; you said you*

wished you could do more flying before we left Earth, and this atmosphere is pretty close to being perfect for flying."

"We have the time, so why not. So what kind of plane can you make? And where can we put a grass field?"

"I can build you any plane you want, and we won't need to disturb any field. I can build you a hovering airport."

"Oh cool. Let's get started. We can start with a P-51 Mustang. When can you build the airport and plane." As soon as I said that, I was standing on the deck of the airport, or carrier. It was a runway and parking area floating in the sky, and on it was a brand-new, shiny P-51 Mustang, ready to go.

"This Mustang is a little different from the original Mustangs. It is beefed up and has twice the horsepower. It still sounds the same as the original but has a totally different engine. It also has something I call a crash field. If you somehow crash, you won't get hurt. You can hit a cliff wall and not get a scratch. And you have unlimited fuel. Do you want something to chase?"

"Maybe later, but this so cool." For the next three hours, I flew around just to get the feel of it. I came back to the runway and landed to have lunch, Athena had attached a diner to the parking area, so I had lunch and got back in the air. Later I had supper at the diner. At twenty-one hundred hours, we beamed everything back to *Stingray*.

I decided to get into the pond and was sitting there thinking. "Athena, can you still track the tanker?"

"Not for much longer. It has made several course corrections. I am still not sure where its final destination is."

"I hope they will contact us. Today was so great. Thank you. That was pretty neat when you joined me."

"You're welcome; I enjoyed it too."

"Athena could I have an ice-cold lager?" One appeared, floating in the air. "Thank you. This so nice. I hope I can still enjoy this after a couple thousand years. But right now, I'm going to enjoy this."

I sat there for another hour and then got up and went to bed.

For the next five weeks, I spent my time flying. The first week started the day after the P-51. I started with a glider, and each day I flew something different. For the rest of the week I stayed with prop planes like the P-38, P-40, and P-61, then a B-25, B-29, and B-35 flying wing. The following week, I piloted jet fighters: the F-86, F-101, F-4, F-14, F-15, F-18 and F-22. The third week, I flew jet bombers. I didn't spend the entire day in any of them expect three: the XB-49, a jet-powered flying wing; the XB-70, which was hard to land—it took two crashes to finally learn how to land it (the crash field worked pretty well); and the B-58, man is that thing fast for flying in this atmosphere—of course this one was slightly modified. During that week, I also flew a couple of passenger planes: the 707, 727, 747, and 787. The fourth week I flew helicopters of all kinds and a V-22. The final week, I flew an X-plane. Athena put a catapult on the hoverport to launch them. And on the last day, I put my new suit to the test. I ran to the edge and dived off; just as my feet left the deck, I hit the thruster and launched myself into the air. I was thinking that the human body was a little unstable flying by itself. Then I saw that I had a hand control in each hand, and I looked out of the corner of my eye and saw wings. I now had one of those jet-powered wings. We later launched an X-15, and I flew it all the way back to *Stingray*. Boy did I get an eyeful; the X-15 looked like a flea approaching a blue whale.

The glider I flew the day after the P-51 had a small jet engine, and I got it up to thirty thousand meters and turned off the engine and glided around up there. It was so serene. Then I remembered about the U-2 and then had Athena turn the glider into a U-2. Flying that was so cool. The part I liked the most was chasing Athena with an F-86 and an F-15. I also raced her in an SR-71. She put me to shame in all three of them.

"That should be enough playing around, time to get back to work," I said. "I could do this for a long time; we have to do this again and with more planes."

CHAPTER THIRTEEN

The Catastrophe

I t took us a little over five days to get to the next system. The star was a red giant, and it had expanded to engulf the inner planets. The outer four were close enough to have had their atmospheres burned away.

We came out of warp about a hundred AU from the system, and the radiation and heat were very intense, but *Stingray* had no problem getting close to the system, owing to its special hull construction.

"I have found signs of a very old civilization, an advanced one at that, dating back at least seventy-five thousand years," Athena said. *"There are signs of a battle on these outer planets. The radiation from the sun has made it difficult to scan anything in any kind of detail. The only way I know that they were advanced is in the way they built their buildings. I don't think the outermost planet had an atmosphere."*

"Any signs of space structure?" I asked.

"Yes, there is a very large debris field on the outermost planet, possibly from a large space station. There is no sign of a main drive unit. The ruins on the other two planets are almost gone. The star started to expand about seventy-five thousand years ago. The First Ones' star chart has a note stating that it was an unnatural expansion, but it's been too long to tell what was added to cause it to expand or how it worked."

"So some exterior force caused the star to expand. Do you have any idea how that was done?"

"No, but whatever it was had to be massive."

"How far to the next star system?"

"About twelve days at warp twenty; it is two hundred seventy-one light years away."

"The stars are kind of sparse out here; I guess it's because we are so close to the edge of the galaxy. The systems we are passing—nothing interesting?"

"I have detail scans of those systems. We don't have to stop at them unless you want to. The next system is interesting because it is a binary star system. I have some star systems that we will come across for us to study during the next twelve days."

"Good," I replied. "I need a break from the elegant squid-people language. I like the way you present the star systems with the holograms; it's like flying in on the system without a ship. Look at the time; it's time for supper."

I appeared by the table, looking out into the biosphere, and started thinking about what I should have for supper. "You know, Athena, I think I will have goulash—a big bowl of goulash with hot garlic bread and an ice-cold stein of lager." The meal appeared. "Thank you, that looks good and smells great."

After supper, Athena and I beamed down to the computer room and started to study star systems. For the next twelve days, we studied the star systems that we passed by. They were interesting, but not enough for us to stop at them. We got everything we needed with the scans; most of the planets had no atmospheres, and a lot were frozen.

On the twelfth day, we arrived at the edge of the system and started to study the binary suns.

"The suns are three hundred eighty million kilometers apart and orbiting a planet at the center of the system," Athena told me. *"The planet is about five times the size of Earth. The suns are not as hot as Earth's sun, but the suns orbit opposite each other, so the planet is in daylight all the time. The planet does have very dense plant life and a very humid atmosphere. There is no animal life. The water is covered up by the plants, so there is no open space. Some of the plants have evolved to breathe oxygen and expel carbon dioxide. There is no place for you to beam down to."*

"No vacation spot. Okay, I won't beam down. What about the outer planets?" I said.

"There are six more planets and an asteroid belt on the outside of the sun's orbit. Regarding the outer planets, there is not much to report. One gas giant is just outside of the circumstellar habitable zone, or Goldilocks zone, and the rest are frozen rocks. Stand by. The plants are not indigenous to that planet. It looks as if they started growing over seventy-five thousand years ago. Something happened in this sector of space about then. This is another unnatural occurrence."

"We need to reexamine those other systems to see if anything happened about seventy-five thousand years ago. How long to that system with the warning beacon?"

"Eight days. That should be enough time to reexamine the systems we won't stop at. Stand by. One of the asteroids in the belt has a very large diamond in it. I can make another billion-carat diamond for our collection, but it will be an Asscher-cut jade-green diamond."

"Okay, why not."

We spent the next eight days reexamining the other system and found out that the two red giants were unnatural but had expanded so much that they had engulfed their planets, but there was no sign of life so far as we could tell. The expansion, however, had happened about seventy-five thousand years before.

Of the systems along the way that we didn't stop at, one encircled a red giant that had expanded about seventy-five thousand years before. We found the wreckage of a small space vessel on a planet just outside of the red giant. The planet had stopped rotating, and the wreck was on the far side of the planet. The wreckage had been there for about seventy-five thousand years.

"Athena, as best I can figure, a civilization that invented a weapon to turn stars into red giants must have tried to conquer this region of space about seventy-five thousand years ago. I wonder what happened to them. The star charts show hardly any civilization in this region. What about this system with the warning beacon?"

"Yes, the warning beacon is issuing a warning not to go beyond here for safety reasons. An advanced culture wants to remain isolated from the rest of the region and will attack vessels. It has one hell of a defense field in place. And it's interfering with my scans. Stand by. Whoa, there are millions of defense drones patrolling this system, and there is some wreckage. I have Stingray at a complete stop at the beacon, and the number of drones in this area is increasing. We would be in a little trouble if we adventured on; they couldn't destroy us, but they could hurt us. The number is still increasing. Wait; there is a large uninhabited planet just outside the defense field that is making these drones as we speak."

"Okay, let's back up and turn around and start making our way to the next system. Keep an eye on them."

"I'll keep a lot of eyes on them. They made a couple thousand of them while we were there. Whatever is there can make drones faster than I can."

"Could they be the First Ones?"

"No, they are older, but they may not be as advanced as the First Ones, or they are not showing it. The First Ones' new beacons have told me a lot about some of their advancement, but not all. We did exchange some data back at the Dragon Keepers' system. Hey, wait a minute; they copied all my recipes. They must have wanted to try your taste in food. Wow, they copied a lot of data that I didn't know at the time, but they didn't try to hide it. I knew they copied the data on the Nebula and what happened in there."

"It's what, a little over seven and a half days to the system where the memory-core shell came from? Did you get to gather any data from that planet making the drones?"

"Yes, it was manned, so to speak, by one of each of thirty-nine different species of creatures. That is about the same number of red giant star systems that formed seventy-five thousand years ago, according to the star charts. This is more than likely the survivors of that catastrophe. They did have a library, and I was able to copy it. It's very large, and it will take some time to translate it. The thing is, it was very easy to copy. As advanced as they are, their library was virtually unguarded, and it was also very old."

"So for the next week we will have to spend time on this library," I said, "translating it and going over it. Maybe we can find out what happened in this sector of space seventy-five thousand years ago. Might as well start out with a good lunch. I think I will have a Dagwood sandwich ... yeah. To the kitchen!"

"Oh no, he's hungry."

After a week of studying the data from that library, I sat down beside Athena in the computer room and listened to her analysis of what may have happened in this sector of space seventy-five thousand years ago.

"The people from the center planet of that binary system—we can call them Medios, meaning 'center'—started warring with their neighbors because they thought they should rule the galaxy. They were advanced enough to do it if they fought one or two civilizations at a time, but they decided to fight them all at once. According to the data, it was about forty civilizations altogether; one is missing. It's not the First Ones; they hadn't started space travel then. It may be the missing civilization that spread the plant life on the binary system's planet, because none of the other civilizations knew who did that. When the civilization from the binary system was forced from their planet, they went into hiding for a long time. The others thought it was for good, but after a couple of hundred years they came back with a very large ship and caused all the stars to become red giants. The survivors got together and had one last battle, and everyone lost. There were very few survivors, and they all gathered on a damage ship, repaired it, and made it to that last system and became isolationists. There are ten planets inside that defense field, and all of them have been terraformed. They all live on those ten planets and have had no wars at all. And as far as they know, there were no survivors from that big ship. There is no reference on where this battle took place or where this ship is. As for the missing civilization, the First Ones have not come across them—or at least they do not say so on their star chart, and they make no reference to the last battle or the giant ship." Athena paused. *"We have arrived at the memory cores' shell planet, and I have started detail scans."*

"Good. I'll have lunch here, and you can tell me the details. I'll have a bowl of beef stew and a tall glass of lager." A table and the food appeared in front of me. "Thank you."

"I found where they got the crystalline material from. It's harder than diamond, and it was grown—grown very slowly, but it was grown. They surgically removed the top of a mountain range and set it in the nearby desert to expose the cavern containing the crystalline material, to expose it to the blue sun. After six hundred years or so, they harvested it. Each time they harvest it, it takes a little longer to grow back. They have harvested it one time since the Nebula has been through—about thirty thousand years

ago. It has now reform a bigger, taller mountain range about double the size. If it's all right, I'm going to harvest a billion cubic meters of it."

"Sure, go ahead," I replied. "So they just cut off the tops of the mountains and set them off to the side to let the sun shine on the crystals, which causes them to grow. Wow. Anything else that is unusual that we haven't come across?"

"We are capable of doing the same. There is a purple diamond inside an asteroid in the asteroid belt orbiting just between this planet and the sun. I can cut it down to the same size to match the other two diamonds we have. We can start collecting Asscher-cut billion-carat diamonds."

"We can? Wow. Yes, why not collect Asscher-cut billion-carat diamonds … no big deal. I guess we have come a long way since we left Earth. We had better start marking them somehow to tell which system they came from. I hate to see what my tax bill will look like."

"I have been using the First Ones' star chart coordinates to mark all the gems and unusual metals."

"So we now have three Asscher-cut billion-carat diamonds in the basement and three diamond bowls of hundred-carat gemstones in my living room. How much time do you need to finish mining the crystal?"

"I'm finished mining. Is there something you would like to do?"

"Are we too close to that blue star? That's a big, hot sun."

"We are fourteen billion kilometers from the blue sun, and Stingray's hull has no problem with the heat. Stingray could be as close as seven billion kilometers before we would start to feel the heat. I detect no temperature change in you."

"No temperature change; that star just looks too hot."

"The temperature of this sun is thirty-four thousand degrees Kelvin; it is very hot."

"How long will it take to get to the liquid memory planet system?"

"Its two thousand three hundred sixty light years away. At warp thirty, we will get there in a little under thirty-two days. We will be doing twenty-seven thousand times the speed of light."

"Is that going to be hard on the engine, or are you going to use the wing engines too?"

"Yes, I will use the wing engines too. All three will run at 70 percent."

"Only 70 percent on all three to get to warp thirty? How much power are we using?"

"The engine is using 45 percent of our power, and the shield is using 15 percent of our power, so they are at 60 percent now. Warp forty is the fastest I think we should go. The engines will be at 95 percent and using fifty percent of our power, and the shield will be at 105 percent and using 35 percent of our power. We could be at Earth in a year and half with a couple of rest stops, but we would miss a lot of sites along the way. We would also be traveling at sixty-four thousand times the speed of light."

"Yeah, it would be nice, I guess, but like you said, we would miss out on a lot of things. Plus, we would scare the heck out of them if we showed up. Let's get underway; I need to get something to eat and then take a swim."

I was standing beside the table, looking through the living room and out into the woods. Athena was hovering in her spot. I sat down at the table, thinking, *What do I want to eat? Something not hot. Ah yes.*

"Athena, can I have a garden salad with crab meat, a corned beef sandwich, and a tall glass of ice-cold lager." Just as I finished asking for it, it appeared. "Thank you."

When I finished, I said, "That was good. Well, we still have a lot to go over, but we can start tomorrow. Now it's time for a swim."

I walked down to the creek and dived in and swam to the other pond and back. I then came back up to the top-level pond and relaxed.

"I'm thinking we may have to build a jogging track that goes around this park," I said.

CHAPTER FOURTEEN

The Survivors

During the thirty-two-day trip, Athena and I went over a lot of data that we had been gathering since we got out of the Nebula. We were also looking at the systems we were passing. We were getting some detail, but just enough to pique our interest and mark the systems for visiting when we had the time. We had to get to the liquid memory system.

Now that we had found civilizations older than the First Ones', we briefly wondered whether we should still call them the First Ones. We decided we should, as they were the first ones to conquer space travel after the red giant star war. There were two civilizations unaccounted for: the ones who started the war and were presumed dead, and the other race who didn't fight in the last battle and who we suspected may be hiding. It must have been some war.

We arrived at the system, and it was like the first system we found. There was only a huge asteroid belt orbiting nothing. The suns were completely destroyed, having left nothing but a void in the middle of this giant asteroid belt. There was no sign of any liquid memory anywhere. We spent the entire day scanning, finding only trace amounts infused with other materials.

"Stand by. Someone has mined it. The First Ones were here a long time ago—shortly after it was destroyed. That's why I didn't see it at first."

"Can you track them to their home world using this trail, or is there a trail?" I asked.

"No trail, but I can use the navigation information from the First Ones' cargo ship by correcting for the time dilation. There I have it. Oh boy, it's about a hundred light years from the fourth star system we visited—the one before the survivors' system. It will take about thirty-three days to get there."

"I do want to stop off at that system—the one where we think we saw floating mountains. Before we leave, is there anything unusual about the systems in this sector of space? Who knows how long it will be before we return to this region."

"Stand by. Scanning."

After a few minutes, Athena replied, *"Yes there is. A system about fifty light years from here shows some unusual water activity. It's flowing upward. We need to get close for a more detailed scan. At warp fifteen, we can be there in five and a half days."*

"Good. We can take it slow for now. How long will it take to get to the floating mountains' system?"

"It will take a little over thirty days at warp thirty; it's one thousand three hundred twenty-six light years away."

"Let's go see this upward-flowing water. This will be interesting to see. But before we go, are there any billion-carat diamonds you'd like to collect?"

"Yes, there are," said Athena. *"There are some large diamonds that have been infused with the memory liquid, making them a rich blue color. Hmm ... I can make these into small storage devices."*

"Go ahead; mine what you want," I said.

"There is another large diamond in another sector of the belt that is turquoise."

"No reason you can't have both," I said, chuckling. "Okay, it's time to eat supper; as soon as you are finished shopping, we can get underway."

We appeared in the biosphere next to my little house. *"I'm not shopping; I'm gathering resources."*

I walked into the living room, and on my way to the table, I noticed another pedestal with another diamond bowl of hundred-carat gemstones, and now all the pedestals had a hundred-carat sapphire-cut diamond imbedded in them.

"Those are some nice storage devices," I said.

"Yes," Athena replied. *"Now they have the complete details of their systems on them. Mining complete. Course set and accelerating to warp fifteen."*

I spent the next five days going over the old civilization library data, learning things about them and their ways of life. The whole time, there have never been any wars between them. There was no space travel; only certain elders were allowed to travel between planets, and they did so by using transporters. Out of those few, only one from each race was allowed to travel to the outer planet, where the only knowledge of the defense shield and drones were kept. They all knew of the great war, the reason they were driven to this system, and the dangers outside of the defense shield. They had been attacked by a lot of civilizations throughout the centuries, but none had been able to beat their drones or shields. Every thousand years, they would debate whether or not to venture out. The move to venture was always overwhelmingly defeated. They could leave but were not allowed to return, and that very rarely happened.

The races knew of each other, but owing to environment conditioning needs, they could not all live together. The visiting elders would live in special compounds with the needed environment conditions and share all knowledge with each other, and they also would help each other with their problems. They would also get together and send probes out to other systems. Their biggest goal was to remain isolationist.

About thirty thousand years ago, before the First Ones started their peacekeeping efforts, there were several civilizations warring with each other. The survivors sent out several hundred peace envoys to help negotiate peace with the warring civilizations. They were all killed, and the survivors took the loss of their envoys as a great tragedy and vowed never to send peace envoys again. Instead, they swore that if anyone came warring near them, they would all be destroyed.

Other races did come several times, and they were all destroyed. After each battle, the debris was cleaned up and stockpiled for future building material. The bodies of their enemies, like their own, were ceremonially cremated into the sun. So when others would come into this section of space knowing of the battles, there was very little debris for them to see that might make them wonder what really happened, or how it happened.

When the First Ones started their peacekeeping efforts, the survivors knew of the First Ones and allowed them to establish boundaries, and they were content to stay within those boundaries that the First Ones set. They had not allowed the First Ones in but would talk to them.

The survivors did not like unnatural death. They saw it as an unacceptable tragedy because they had eliminated all sickness, deformity, and disease. There were no unwanted or accidental births among them. They now had a form of population control that was reasonable and acceptable. Accidents and crime were very rare and were considered a worldwide tragedy.

"Apart from being isolationist and made up of thirty-nine races, they have the perfect multicivilization," Athena said. *"They have made it work for over seventy thousand years, with no signs of it breaking down."*

"They made it out of necessity. I guess they have a good reason to become isolationist. If I lost everything like they did, I would be a little hesitant to venture out too."

"We have arrived at the system we wanted to see. Starting to scan. Hmm, that is interesting. Bringing up the hologram. It is a two-level continent, with the upper level supported by mountain ranges and having a lot of holes to let the sunlight and water though to the lower level. The ocean to the west of the continent has a submerged continent that has volcanoes with vents of hydrogen that is infused into the water, giving it an extra hydrogen molecule—but not permanently. With the heat, the water rises to form massive rain clouds and the third hydrogen molecule is released. Its rain on the upper level forms lakes and rivers, which leak into the lower level. There is so much evaporation that it looks as if water is flowing upward."

"Are there any life forms?"

"Abundant marine life and some plant life, but it's fairly new. Ah, I see why. It seems that occasionally, when the hydrogen builds up, something ignites it, causing a worldwide flash fire, burning off some of the vegetation. There is some animal life, and it has adapted to protect itself from these flash fires, and so have some of the plants.

The fires don't last very long, because it rains here a lot. But it doesn't seem possible for anything to be dry enough to cause fire with these clouds, doesn't seem possible, oh wait. Ah ... lightning, it seldom occurs, but that is the trigger. It ignites the hydrogen and causes flash fires."

"Okay," I said, "have you scanned the rest of the system? Any intelligent life forms here?"

"Not at this time, but there are signs of mining on several of the other planets. I have taken note of what they are mining for. They are after quick and easy deposits of certain materials, and some of them are gemstones; but they have not tried hard enough or long enough to get at the really good ones, and they are very messy."

"I wonder where they go to trade them?"

"Gee whiz, they need to work on their engines. Anybody can follow this trail; it's in the general direction we are going to go. The star chart shows a large space station about seven hundred twenty-three light years away; I'm detecting a large number of metal objects in that area. At warp thirty, we will be there in just under ten days. I suggest we approach with caution until we have a detailed scan of the area."

"How close can you get to them without being detected?"

"I could be right outside their hatch without being detected unless someone looked out the viewport."

Trying not to chuckle, I said, "Yes, I know. Is there something we can hide behind so they can't see us until we can get a good detail scan of that sector of space?"

"Yes, we can approach from behind a planetoid that will keep us out of sight until we can get a good detail scan. Once we are ready to approach them, I can do what I did at the first space station and give them a false signal to follow."

"Okay, we might as well get started. Set course and accelerate to warp thirty."

During the next eight days, we went over the scan Athena did on the three space stations that were at the Nebula, trying to learn all we could about the other races.

On the morning of the ninth day, we approached the station from behind the planetoid and started a detail scan. Athena scanned everything and everyone. We spent the rest of the day going over the scans. We learned that this trading post was just like the first one was—run by the same race, with the same race as guards, with the same rules. In other words, greed was the main motivator; anything goes, to make a profit as long as it looked legal and one didn't get caught unless one had the funds to pay one's way out of it.

"Okay, Athena, how do you suggest I enter the station?"

"I will have a holographic ship approach an outer air lock and dock. Once they open the outer hatch, I will turn out the lights and you can transport in, and we will figure it out as we go."

"Will you bring in *Stingray?*"

"Yes, I will make it look like the ship came out of a hangar deck."

Athena had *Stingray* approach the station with a false signal so as not to alarm the station; she used the same signal as with the first station.

A signal coming from the station said, **"State your purpose."**

"We're here to establish trade," replied Athena.

"We have no docks big enough for you," said the station.

"We will use a shuttle to dock," replied Athena.

"Very well. Use dock twenty-one seventeen. There will be a fee." The station sent the coordinates to the dock.

She then had the holographic depart *Stingray* and docked at the air lock. The outer hatch opened and the lights went out, and it was very dark in the air lock. I appeared in the air lock, and the lights came on. The guard at the viewport just snarled, closed the outer hatch, and cycled the air. Once the air was cycled, the inner hatch opened. I stepped out, and my helmet retracted into my collar. A little humanoid about a meter tall in a robe stepped forward with a device in hand.

The translator in my earpieces translated, "Permit."

I reached into my side pocket and pulled out the strip of metal Athena had given me and stuck it out for it to see. He touched it with his device, and his eyes widened a little.

He leaned over to his guard, a big brute of a humanoid creature with four arms—very muscular, with an ugly face—and whispered something. Athena translated, "That's the purest I've ever seen." He straightened, taking the strip of metal back up, and spoke to me. "Permit accepted for both ship and fine for turning out the lights. What do you have to trade?"

A crowd had started to gather. I reached around with my right hand to the side of my backpack and pulled out the gemstone Athena had given me. This time his eyes almost popped out. He touched it with his device and said, "It's real." Just then, four creatures from my left rushed me.

Athena told me to push out my left arm as if I were pushing them away. I did, and they went flying backward; she had used my shield to repel them. The crowd took a step back, including the administrator and his guard. From my right, three creatures drew their weapons and started pulling their triggers, but nothing happened. Athena told me to swap hands with the gemstone and reach out with my right hand open and then close it. I did, and the weapons came together, and then they were crushed and fell to the floor. This time the crowd took several steps back. Now more guards were coming into the area and forming a half circle in front of me.

The administrator looked at the gemstone and said, "We do not want your kind here. Your permit is revoked. No refund."

My earpiece translated what the three creatures were shouting: "You must pay for our weapons!"

I replied, "That is the price of my friendship."

They looked at each other and shouted back, "We do not want your friendship!"

"Sorry, no refunds," I replied

The administrator stopped and turned around and stared heavily at the gemstone. "What do you want?" he asked.

"A copy of your data libraries."

"You are one of them ... you seek knowledge." He reached for the gemstone.

I pulled the gem away a little. "All of them on the station."

He hesitated and then grabbed the gem. "Deal. Now go."

I turned and entered the air lock. The hatch closed, the air lock started to cycle, my helmet deployed itself, the outer hatch opened, and I stepped into the holographic ship, than I appeared next to Athena in the computer room. Athena then had the holographic ship come back to *Stingray*.

Several ships closed in on *Stingray*. Athena started scanning them very closely and determined they were no threat. When they came to a stop, Athena used *Stingray*'s shields to push them away. They got the message and moved off.

Stingray sat there, and Athena used a false signal to let them think they could see us slowly copying the station's data libraries. Athena, before I even went over to the station had copied not only the station data libraries but also all the other ship's data. While this was happening, Athena set up a hologram image of the inside of the station and we took a tour of the place and all the ships.

After several hours, we finished our tour. We did find the ship that was in the system we had just come from, and they were doing pretty well with the haul they had made from that system. They could have done better if they had put a little more effort into it; they had just missed the mother lode, if they just put another couple of days of work into it. By the way it looked, they did make a good score on what they got. We also found out that the best speed they could do was warp ten, and that was pushing it. It had taken them almost nine months to get back to the station. We thought they should use some of those gems to get some work done on their engines, but it didn't look as if that was going to happen.

We started to leave the area, and when we got far enough away, we went to warp ten. We noticed that one of the ships that had approached us earlier started to follow us. Athena dropped the false signal and went to warp thirty. The ship that was following us started a full sensor scan; to them, we just disappeared. After a while they gave up and went back to the station.

For the next twenty days, Athena and I went over the data we had gathered at the station, studying the races and their so-called laws. They were quite content in not warring with anybody but just swindling them out of their goods. Some races were better at it than others, and if they could get away with it without really upsetting the other party, all the better. The First Ones did keep the peace most of the time, but sometimes a small skirmish did go by unnoticed.

Now I saw why the survivors did what they did. Before the First Ones started their peacekeeping efforts, we learned of a war that started with several of these civilizations that also ended badly for them and set them back a few thousand years. That's why the First Ones decided to engage in their peacekeeping efforts; they didn't want another great war, as this time no one may have survived it. The fear of an advanced civilization using their power to enforceby moving entire fleets with no memory of the move or the place they had been moved from. The small skirmishes were rare, and the swindling was kept to a minimum. The stations out the farthest were the worst.

CHAPTER FIFTEEN

Home World

After traveling 1,326 light years from the liquid memory system, we arrived at the system with the planet that had the floating mountains. Athena started detail scans of the system. Just as we were approaching the edge of the system, Athena brought *Stingray* to a stop.

"There is a warning beacon," she said. *"It just became active. It's a short-range beacon. Probably so as not to draw attention. It says to leave this system alone—to not enter. The second planet that has the floating mountains is in the Goldilocks zone, and so are the third and fourth planets. This is interesting: the third and fourth planets are orbiting each other while orbiting the sun, and they are as close to each other as the Earth and the moon and are the size of Mars."*

Athena continued. *"The second planet is full of life forms—marine, plant, and animal. There may be intelligent life. I'm now using only passive scans on the second planet. My detail scans cause something with the plant life. There are life forms everywhere: land, sea, and air. There are no buildings—none that I can detect. No signs of space travel."*

"Can you bring a holographic image up?" I asked.

"Yes. It will be looking down onto it."

"Wow, that is a lot of plant life. Did you see that? It looks like someone swinging in the trees—and those are some towering trees, like redwoods."

Athena homed in on it. *"Yes, it is a humanoid about two meters tall, and just coming into sight are tree houses and rope bridges. Zooming in on the floating mountains. There are some movement of the mountains, though not much. They seem to stay in this large canyon. Ah, some of the mountains' bottoms match the landscape of the canyon floor. The mountain hovers only about eighty meters above the floor of the canyon. There are several of these canyons with floating mountains existing around this world."*

Athena continued her report. *"The third and fourth planet ... I can only use a passive scan also. I'm afraid I will disturb their orbit by using a detail scan from this range. Their magnetic fields are very fragile; besides, I think the beacon won't let me. When I tried using a detail scan earlier, not only did I get a reaction from the plants, but I also got a reaction from the beacon."*

"Okay, I think we have done enough here, so we might as well get underway, I said. "So you think you know where the home world of the First Ones is. I wonder what they will do when we show up or if they let us show up. Who knows; they may stop us or reroute us. So are you ready? Oh, how long will it take us to get their home world?"

"Twenty days. Stand by. There is a rouge planet, a gas giant about three times bigger than Jupiter, about halfway there. I would like to run a detail scan on it. It's traveling at three quarters of light speed."

"Okay, what makes it so interesting?"

"The moon orbiting it may have structures on it."

During the next ten days, I got into a routine of getting up at seven-thirty and having breakfast. Then, at eight, Athena and I would stroll through the woods thinking of what we could go over that day. Than we would beam down to the computer room and go over what we had discussed earlier. At noon I would have lunch in the computer room, and we would then continue with the analysis, and about three we would beam up to the biosphere and I would snack on some fruit and watch the rain. After the rain, we would beam up to the observatory. About six we would beam back down to the house and I would have supper. After supper, I would usually go for a swim, and about nine-thirty we would go over what we had passed. About eleven-thirty I would go take a shower and go to bed.

On the tenth day, Athena reported, *"We are approaching the rouge planet. Slowing Stingray and going into orbit. Starting detail scan."*

After a few minutes, I asked, "Athena, you find anything?"

"Oh yes. This planet's moon was inhabited even after it left its orbit. Many of the inhabitants survived, and they knew it was coming. There was evidence of mass construction of bunkers and reinforcement of buildings and of launch bunkers—hundreds of them. The planet was able to keep its atmosphere for about two hundred fifty years after the event. The moon then ran into a meteor shower. That was almost eight hundred years ago. It looks like some of the ships launched shortly afterward. I am looking for them now. The meteors did a lot of damage; it looks as though they left before they wanted to. They had to leave a lot of containers behind. The containers are full of works of art and books and things."

"Athena, can you tell what kind of culture they had? Were they peaceful or warring?"

"There appears to be no weaponry, no battle damage, and no sign of forced captivity, but there are signs of art everywhere: statues, paintings, and sculptures. Some of them have been destroyed by the meteor strikes. Stand by. I think I found some

kind of computer storage system. It's mechanical. I can beam it aboard and repair it, but it is quite large. Actually it is a small building—two floors and a hundred meters by a hundred meters. I found another mechanical computer in pieces in a container; it looks like they were going to put it on a ship but ran out of time. I can put it on a hover-platform and dock it next to your house for you to examine."

"Okay."

Athena repaired the mechanical computer and transferred and translated the data to the monitor, and we went over it all. It was copies of music, poetry, manuscripts, and paintings—all sorts of works of art.

"They seemed to be very peaceful people. What happened to them?"

"They left in atomic rocket ships. There are a lot of launch tubes; some are badly damaged. I'll start to scan for them."

"How long ago did they leave?"

"I think I found them about seven hundred light years from here; there're just coasting—hundreds of them. We can get to them in four days at warp forty. They are heading for a system, but they wouldn't get there until a thousand years from now at their present speed, and I think it's the wrong one."

"I think we should try to help them if we can."

"Agreed. What about the other containers? And there are some works of art that they were going to try to save?"

"Can you beam them aboard without damaging them? They are probably very delicate."

"Yes, about 90 percent of the containers are intact, and the rest I can repair. I can reinforce them all too,"

"Okay, let's go get them. We're ready to see how these engines hold up. If you have everything you need from here, then let get going."

After two days at warp forty, Athena slowed *Stingray* almost to a stop.

"Are we slowing down?"

"Yes, I found one of the ships; it's damaged."

Just then a rocket ship appeared in the bay and we picked up speed again. The ship looked like one of the atomic rocket ships from a fifties science fiction movie but was a lot bigger. This ship had been damaged by a meteor that had ripped a gash along the side. The ship had enough power to operate the suspended animation chambers for a couple of more weeks and that was all. Athena repaired the ship and replenished the reactor when she beamed it aboard. We found two more ships that were also damaged and whose engines had finally failed, but a third one wasn't so lucky; all on board had perished. Athena beamed the ship and all its pieces into the transporter buffer. At the end of the fourth day, we rendezvoused with the ships and started scanning.

"Athena, how are they doing?" I asked.

"The ships are all very low on power—maybe forty-five days' worth. Once I beam them aboard, I can replenish their reactors and do some needed repairs. They would not have made it to that planet, plus it wouldn't sustain them. I did find a planet that would sustain them about six hundred light years from here, and we could be there in less than four days, but we would have to rearrange a little and leave all of the cargo containers behind. We can come back for them later. But we can manage."

"What kind of rearranging?" I replied.

"We would have to put the biosphere into the buffer, along with the bridge, the upper deck, and some of the containers. Your apartment would need to be put in an alcove, and you would have to stay in your apartment for the duration. I will stack them in here like matchsticks, and we will just have enough room for all of them after I

transport some sections of the ships into the buffer too. I do not want to put the section of the ship with the suspended animation chambers in the buffer."

"Okay, let's get this done. The faster we get it done, the faster we can get our home back together."

It took Athena a little over six hours to get everything done. She wasn't kidding about stacking the ships like matchsticks, and there was no room to move around in. Athena and my apartment were tightly fitted in an alcove on the side of the bay. Athena added a little deck to the apartment so I could come out and talk to her every once in a while. Athena held all the ships in place with damping and structure fields. She had the builder drones build a container ship to hold all the cargo containers—those she didn't put in the buffer—along with the mechanical computer building and the drones. It was an odd-looking ship, but it would keep them together and not let anyone take them. She had the container ship set a course to the planet. With all the fields at maximum, it could do warp twenty and would join us in twenty-seven days.

Three and a half days later, we were orbiting the planet. For those three days, Athena and I went through their history. They were peaceful people, never warring among themselves. They were somewhat humanoid and had a tail, three eyes, ten fingers, four thumbs, backward knees, and ugly feet that looked like six-toed chicken feet.

The planet was ideal for them—a little smaller than their moon, but their moon was three times the size of Earth. The air and water were almost perfect. The days were a little longer and the gravity was a little lighter then their original planet. The sun was just right. There was some harmful plant life, but nothing deadly. The animal life on this continent was not harmful but plentiful. But on the other continent, there was some that was deadly. The winters would not be too bad, and the summers not that hot; they would have no problem adapting to this planet's climate. They did have six moons—some big and some small.

Athena found a field the size of Kansas and picked a level spot to place everything. She divided a large square of it into nine sections. She then prepped the north, west, east, and south sections for the placing of the ships—about 140 per section.

The ships were designed to land on their tails and then lower themselves down, but Athena thought the design was hurriedly done and the chance of accident was too great, so we put the ships on the ground already lowered. There were 560 ships that launched from the planet with a hundred people on board. Sixteen ships had twenty extra chambers on board. Two ships were lost, and the one that had perished, Athena placed off to the side of the others. All the bodies were still in their chambers but were dead. So 56,020 had survived.

Of the original six hundred launch tubes with ships, forty were destroyed, and hundreds of thousands of people were killed by the meteor strike. They had been planning on ten waves of ships, but the strike ended that. A week after the strike, the moon lost its atmosphere, and right after that, the ships launched with the remaining people. Over half a million people survived the planet leaving its system after its sun died. Now only a little over fifty-six thousand survived. There were hundreds of ships that were built and hundreds more under construction, but with little power and most of the people dead, what they had in the launch tubes was it. But they could take only what was needed.

Winter was coming, and the tents they had were okay but would have made for a very frosty winter. So Athena placed hundred-man barracks beside each ship. They could hook these structures up to their ships for power. And each barrack had a book that had the planet's information in it, in their language. Athena had also placed serval mobile scaffolding structures that they had designed to aid in the disassembly of the ship—about four per section. Athena placed the stricken ship in the northeast section, hoping that it wouldn't freak them out too badly.

Athena started monitoring the suspended animation chambers to make sure they would revive their occupants correctly. She had to correct several of them. After a while they started coming out of their ships and seeing the sunlight; then they saw the barracks and were taken somewhat aback. After a while, they started taking samples of water, soil, and plants. Some of them started going inside the barracks. After a few minutes, they all came out carrying the books with them to show to the others. They started passing the books around, and then, one by one, they started looking up.

"Athena, can they see us?" I asked.

"It's possible. Uh oh, they are pointing at us."

"I think we'd better get behind one of the moons for now."

Just then a group had discovered the stricken ship and was calling them all over.

That was our cue to leave. We got behind the closest moon and sent in several small probes to monitor them to see how they were adapting to their new world. With the probes in position, we left the system to rendezvous with the container ship and bring back their containers. We rendezvoused with the ship and beamed everything back on board. Athena kept the container ship intact and placed it in the cargo bay. Just in case, when we got back we stayed out of their line of sight at first. We started thinking of ways to bring back their containers. We finally decided to beam them down using sparkly effects and sound. We moved into an orbit right over them.

First Athena beamed down using the effects and announced, *"Please stand clear of the red area."* Athena lit up the area in red light in the southwest section. *"We are beaming down your containers."* She started beaming down the containers and building with a light and sound show. During the beaming, nobody ran away; they all stayed and watched. Once it was over, they cheered, and then they pointed to the building and shouted with joy.

Athena then announced, *"Beam-down is complete."*

After a few days, we decided that they were doing fine. And we were happy with having our home back together. So we decided to do a low-orbit flyby. They seemed to be okay with it. On the way out, we picked up a signal. It was coming from the planet.

Athena translated: *"From the Children of Hope, we thank you."*

"Athena, tell them we are sorry for their loss and hope this helps in some way."

Just as we were leaving the system, we saw a beacon.

"Darn, didn't even see it get placed," Athena said.

"That reminds me; you did write in the book that they should be cautious of other races and that there is a protector in this sector of space."

"Yes."

After a couple of weeks of cruising to the First Ones' home world, we got about one light year out and slowed to warp ten. Athena started scanning.

"I'm not picking up anything. Nothing. Not a darn …

The universe blinked.

"Oh no, I think we found them; did they teleport us somewhere?" I asked.

"Yes, scanning now, oh wow."

"I've got you saying it now," I said. "What did you find?"

CHAPTER SIXTEEN

Another New Home

"*It's a battlefield—or what is left of one,*" Athena said. "*It must cover at least a light year in diameter; there are a lot of ships here—I mean a lot. It's hard to tell the difference between ships, with so much debris. There is one ship that is huge—I mean really huge. You know how you felt when you approached Stingray in the X-15?*"

"Yeah, I felt pretty small, like really, really tiny."

"*Yeah, that sounds about right. That's about the way I feel right now. This thing is huge. The overall length of this thing is about twenty-eight thousand kilometers. The forward cylinder is about twelve thousand kilometers long and six thousand kilometers in diameter—almost twice the diameter of the Moon, and then that is connected to a sphere about twelve thousand kilometers in diameter—almost as big as Earth. Earth is twelve thousand seven hundred forty-two kilometers. At the opposite end of the sphere is another cylinder about four thousand kilometers long and four thousand in diameter—just a little bigger then the diameter of the Moon. The Moon*" *is three thousand four hundred seventy-five kilometers. The forward cylinder has a two-thousand-kilometer-diameter tunnel all the way to the sphere, and it is badly damaged. There are holes in this thing that Stingray could fly around in. This could take a couple of days to scan. While we are waiting on the scans, we can do the modification to the bio—wait ... what in the world? It's gone. For crying out loud they took the whole biosphere this time. At least they left your house. I guess they figured that since we were going to redo some of the biosphere, we might as well redo the whole thing. Hold on; they took the drones too. I'm checking my diamonds. Oh, I have an extra one. I guess they paid for it this time with a diamond—instead of a star chart like they gave us when we came out of the Nebula and they took the forest out of the buffer. That's neat; this diamond floats, and it has an orange tint to it."*

"Well, I guess we can start with a clean slate for this twelve-hundred-fifty-acre plot," I said. "This time we will just use force fields instead of a dome. Can you still make it rain?"

"Oh yes, I can even make it snow if you want." She brought up a hologram of the upper deck of the computer room.

"Great. What about lighting? The floating light panel should work. Now put the land on the deck. Okay. Now make the hilltop where the house goes about fifty-five meters in elevation. Nice. Let's make the pond about three times as wide and about four times as long, and make the hilltop big enough for it. Great. Now make the area for the other ponds twice as big, 'cause we're going to make the ponds twice as big. And you'd better make the slope more gradual too. Nice. Now put in the ponds and waterfalls. That's nice. Before you put in the small lake, let's bring up the level of the land by the north wall to about a hundred meters in elevation with the slope about the same. Oh, that looks great. Now the northeast corner—bring it out in a two-hundred-meter-wide strip to about even with the end of the slope, and make the west-side slope about one-third as steep as the others, but have the end of the strip come straight down to make a waterfall at this corner from a ten-meter-wide creek running down the middle of the strip. That looks really nice. Now put a small lake at the base of the waterfall. Make it about twelve acres, and have a creek connecting this bottom pond to that lake. Great. Now, in the exact middle, place a tower a hundred meters tall with an observation deck big enough for you and me to be on. Wow, that's high. Make it about 10 percent bigger. Okay, now for handrails." I stuck out my arms to find a comfortable position. "About this high for the rails. Okay, you can put in the trees and put a short wall along the sides for the berry bushes. And could I have a clear line of sight to the waterfall from my house? That looks really nice, Athena. Excellent job. Oh, a nice breeze too. Now what else can we put in here? Hmm."

"How about a jogging track around the park? You could use it to do some exercising. You need to do something."

"Okay, start at the house and go in between the short wall and the pond. Wait, put a rock formation about a meter high in between the wall and the pond, along the whole width of the pond, and you can use it as the water source for the pond. And put a bridge over the pond's end. I guess you will have to put in a couple other bridges down here and over by the creek, by the waterfall. Have it go up the hill along the top and then down close to the side, and then zigzag back to this first bridge. Make it about ten klicks."

"How's that?"

"Wow, that looks great. How long will you need to build it?"

"Stand by ... (after a brief pause) There, it's complete," said Athena.

"Can we go up to the house now?" In the blink of an eye we were there. "Thank you. I really like this little house. I'm not taxing you any, am I?" I said.

"Not at all. While I was doing this, I also made a couple hundred drones to help me with the scanning out there. As you say, "No biggie."

"Okay, I think I'll have a steak dinner and then relax in the cement pond and go to bed. Beautiful job, Athena. This looks so nice, and the wonderful thing about it is that we can always add to it."

The lights dimmed, and Athena was stationary beside the pond. I dried off and put on my clean underwear and walked into the living room. There I went across the deck to the railing and looked out into the bay.

Athena glided up beside the house. *"What are you thinking about?"*

"Nothing really. Just looking out into the bay. Over half of those containers are filled with elements unknown on Earth." I tapped on the force field. "Athena, do we really need these fields?"

"Oh yes, some of these elements smell pretty bad, and a couple of these containers are made of those elements so as to contain some very unusual elements. Are you sure you want me to open up the field?" A portal about a meter in diameter became visible in front of me, and the air hit me right in the nose.

"Oh my, that smell is pretty powerful," I said

The portal closed. *"Those are some of the new elements I found. Here, take some breaths through this."*

A breathing mask appeared in front of me, hovering in the air, I took it and started breathing through it. It smelled like mint, which was refreshing to say the least. The mask then disappeared.

"Okay, that stays on this side of the galaxy, and we will keep the force field just for the smell. Wow."

I made my way to my bedroom and crawled into bed. It started to rain.

"That's nice, Athena. Thank you, and good night." I fell asleep.

The next morning, I woke up to find Athena in her usual spot.

"Good morning, Athena, how's everything?"

"All systems are operating perfectly. I should be finished with my scans by tomorrow morning. What would you like for breakfast?"

"Biscuits and sausage gravy, four sausage links, a mug of coffee, tomato juice, and a fresh orange from this bowl." After I finished eating, I grabbed another orange and walked over to Athena. "How about beaming down to the computer room and seeing what is happening out there."

We beamed down to the computer room, and Athena brought up a hologram of the space in front of us.

"Nothing, really, is happening."

"That is one big ship and the damage it took." I peeled my orange and looked for a trash can; and then I remembered there were no trash cans. I held out the peelings and Athena dematerialized them and then I ate my orange.

"Yes, even with all that damage you think there would be some data left in something. But there is no data anywhere—nothing. I think it's all been erased. So far everything I have scanned has had no data on it. Something should have survived, but there is nothing. Someone must have erased it. It wasn't the First Ones; it happened about seventy-five thousand years ago. Oh yeah, this is the great battle that the survivors survived; that much I do know. The only people I know that could have done this is the survivors; they must have not wanted anyone to get this technology. But I will keep looking. I also think this is the ship that caused all the suns to become red giants; it's the only ship big enough to cause that."

"Good orange, Athena. Fantastic job on the fruit trees. So this is the great battle that's in the data from the survivors. That's a lot of ships out there—an awful lot."

For the rest of the day, I watched Athena scanning each piece of debris and trying to piece together the ships. It was like putting together a giant puzzle, but Athena did it a lot faster. Just before noon, I had a big hoagie and a tall stein of lager.

"Good sandwich, and I like the ice crystals you have in the lager."

We continued with the piecing together of the ships together to see if we could get a rough estimate of how many ships there were in this debris field, as big as it was. Athena also started making more scans of the planetary debris, as she had found something strange about it. Finding all the pieces to the gigantic ship was a chore; we did it to get an idea of what this ship looked like.

Around eighteen hundred we beamed back up to the house. I went for a jog around the park. I stripped off everything except my underwear and started barefoot around the track.

"I like this material you made the track out of; it's softer than sand—more like a powder, but it leaves no dust clouds. I guess I should start making this a routine. What do you think, Athena?"

"It wouldn't hurt, and if you get bored with it, I can always add obstacles to it. Would you like me to preheat the pond?"

"Yes, to about thirty-eight degrees Celsius. You have about twenty minutes to do it. That should be enough time for you."

"Please, I'm already done. Would you like a cooler breeze?"

"This is just fine, thank you. Here comes that hill."

After I rounded the last corner, I headed straight for the pond and jumped in.

"This feels great! Thanks, Athena. That sure looks great with that big hill and the waterfall back there, and this breeze sure is nice and smells good too. These ponds with the waterfalls sure are something. It's nice to listen to at night. And all these fruit trees really help make it smell so fresh in here, but don't open the field. Okay, for supper I'll have salad, spaghetti with garlic bread, and a glass of red wine—any one of those sweet red wines you came up with when you were trying to replicate wine. Some of those were pretty good. And for dessert, a bowl of berries with whipped cream. I almost forgot about those berries."

"You know all these wines, lagers, and hard drinks are nonalcoholic," Athena said.

"They are? Well, as long as they taste this good, I don't care; that's why the scotch is so smooth. You have this replicating thing down pat."

"I learned a lot from all those civilizations' replicators, plus I had a lot of world-famous recipes, with some top-notch chefs' tips. Then we practiced a lot for more than a month."

"Yeah, I remember that; I gained about ten pounds then," I said while making my way to the pond. "With artificial gravity, I was able to take it off. Seriously, I was so thankful that we were able to get artificial gravity. I did not like zero Gs; it made me queasy all the time. Could you bring up a hologram up while I sit in the pond?"

I got in the upper pond and waded over to the edge of the waterfall and looked over. The waterfall had a wall that was just a couple of centimeters below the surface to let a thin sheet of water go over the edge. "This water is nice, Athena. Can you put a submerged lounger right next to the wall here, low enough to have the water go over my shoulders about a centimeter?" The edge of the waterfall's wall morphed into a lounger, and I sat down in it. "Great, just right. That feels good."

I sat there, relaxing and watching the hologram, and my music started playing. "Athena, this is the life."

The universe blinked.

CHAPTER SEVENTEEN

The Great Battle

"Uh oh, now what did they do?" I said.

"Uh oh is right. We are right in the middle of the battle seventy-five thousand years ago; they transported us back in time."

"Beam us to the computer room," I said a bit excitedly.

We appeared in the computer room, me dressed and dried. Just then *Stingray* shook violently and I almost fell to the floor.

"Shield on full. Hold on!"

Again we got hit. This time it was twice as hard, and the shields were vaporized. The first strike had been meant for a smaller ship that we appeared in front of.

"Replacing shields. There was no damage to Stingray."

I looked at the hologram. "Athena, I think we are sitting in the middle of a big gun barrel. I think we should move."

"No kidding. I'm trying, but everyone is shooting at us. Uh oh, they are charging their main weapon. The others are losing; that gigantic ship is taking them out. Half their fleet is destroyed." As she got *Stingray* moving along the side of the ship, we were only two thousand meters from the surface of that gigantic ship.

"Can you cause that ship's weapon to overload?" I asked.

"Maybe, if I can get through their internal shields. It's a good thing we are inside of their main shield. Ah, I found a way in. Scanning. Found the main hardware for charging the weapon. Searching."

Meanwhile, we got hit three more times. Twice Athena was able to replace the shields. The initial blast caused the shields to literary blow up, sending most of the energy back into the gigantic ship, causing some damage. The third time, Athena didn't get the shield up in time, and *Stingray*'s hull was able to cause the blast to bounce back into the ship, but it shook *Stingray* very violently.

"Athena, please hurry." Another hit struck. "How long can you keep this up?" I asked.

"Unknown."

"One more thing: if it's not too much trouble, can you scan everything?" I asked.

"Already doing that."

"That's my girl."

"Thank you. I found it. They wouldn't be able to get to this part in time. Stand by. They keep changing their frequency. They're on to me. Stand by ... Got it. I suggest we get out of here."

About ten seconds later, an explosion erupted. That big hole that Athena said we could fly *Stingray* around in? We caused it.

"Do you think they have a chance now?" I asked.

"They may. I can see why there was no winner in this battle; that thing is still putting out a lot of firepower. Most of their secondary guns are still firing. They must have their own power source."

Even with that big explosion, the ship did not break apart. The sphere section was severely damaged. With its main power source gone, they no longer had their main weapon. They still were able to put up a fight with most of their secondary weapons. Their main shields were gone also, but they still had a lot of their secondary shields but were slowly losing. Without their main shield, the weapons of the thirty-nine civilizations were getting through.

Just then, there were a couple more hits. Athena couldn't get the second shield up fast enough. *Stingray* shook violently again.

"Who is shooting at us now?" I said. "Can't they see we were helping them? Not very grateful, are they?"

"It's a big Dreadnought after us—one of the thirty-nine civilizations'."

"Shouldn't he be helping fire at that ship? Is there anything more we can do?"

"Not really. I'm going to max warp."

Just then the universe blinked again.

"Now where are we?"

"Checking ... We are back in our own time. Checking for damage."

"Did *Stingray* sustain any?"

"No. The hits we received without shields bounced off the hull, but we could have taken only a couple more shots before it started to do damage."

"Did we get anything with the scans?"

"Some. I had a hard enough time just getting through that ship's shield, let alone anyone else's shields. Their shields were a totally different type of shield. It will take a few hours to adjust my scanners just in case we encounter them again. Wait; stand by. Wow, I have been given an updated database. Wow, I have a new star chart with a lot

of data on each star system, including this one. It will take me a while to examine this new data. I should be ready by noon tomorrow if there are no more battles to assist in."

"Well, hopefully they won't do any more tonight; that's enough excitement for one night. I think it's time to turn in."

Just like that I was standing next to my bed and Athena was in her usual spot. I took off my clothes and crawled into bed, and it started to rain as usual; it was so nice and peaceful.

"No forward hologram. After what just happened, I don't need that ship staring at me tonight."

"I can give you another direction to view. How's' this?"

"That's fine. Good night, Athena."

"Good night."

CHAPTER EIGHTEEN

The Aftermath

I woke up the next morning. It was a great morning; the air smelled great, and the breeze was really refreshing.

"Good morning, Athena. How are you doing this fine morning? No new battles, are there?"

"Good morning. No new battles. And it is a very good morning."

"This morning I think I well have a pork steak, two eggs over easy, hash browns, toast, a mug of coffee, and that citrus juice drink you came up with." The feast appeared. "That looks great. Thank you."

Just as I was going to cut into my steak, I paused and looked around.

"Just wondering if they were going to do anything."

"Not yet. I think it's safe to eat your breakfast. No, wait ... No, it's safe; go ahead."

After breakfast, Athena and I went to the computer room and studied the events of the previous night. After a few hours of studying the new data, we knew what that gigantic ship looked like, plus all the others.

"Okay I would like to go up to the house and have a big, hearty lunch and then go stretch out in the grass and watch you go over the data."

We went up to the house, and I went into the kitchen and sat at the table and had a rack of ribs, potato salad, and coleslaw, with two steins of ice-cold lager.

I lay there watching the hologram Athena had put up, and I think I drifted off to sleep a couple of times; then I sat up because Athena was reviewing our encounter.

"That ship looked bigger in one piece," I said. "The firepower that thing had ..."

"Stand by ... It didn't shoot something at the stars; it took certain elements from the stars, causing them to expand into red giants. Their main weapon was twofold; it would draw the elements out of the stars and later be used to shoot an energy burst that would destroy a lot of ships or a planet. I think we got there right after the second shot. It destroyed all those ships with two shots, and I think it destroyed that sun with one shot. That's what drew everyone here; it was destroying this system."

I stood up and brushed myself off and stepped closer to the hologram. "Athena, could I get a tall table and a tall glass of lemonade with ice cubes?" The items appeared. "Thank you."

After a couple more hours of watching the hologram, I looked at Athena and said, "Athena, that's enough for me for now. I'm going for a jog and have supper." As I turned, the glass and table disappeared. I walked up to the house, stripped down, and went for a run.

After the run, I got into the pond and relaxed. After an hour, I got out and got dressed and then entered the kitchen and sat at the table. I thought for a moment. "Athena, I would like to try your meatloaf with macaroni and cheese, green beans, and a tall glass of milk. For dessert I will have a big slice of apple pie."

After supper, I walked back over to Athena's side and started watching the hologram again. The debris field was a light year in diameter, and Athena was scanning every millimeter of it. I was planning to watch only an hour of scans before going into the pond, but I ended up watching almost three hours before I realized it. I got into the pond and sat on my submerged lounger, relaxing. I was just about to ask when Athena placed the hologram in front of me. Before I knew it, it was twenty-three hundred, so I slid down the slide and got under the waterfall and washed myself. I then walked up to the house and walked into the bedroom. By the time I got there, I was dry, so I put on my underwear, got into bed, and was lying there when I started laughing.

"What is so funny?"

"I was just thinking what my mother would say if she knew that I no longer have to pick my clothes up because they just disappear and reappear all cleaned, pressed, and hung up. she used to say, 'Clothes won't magically clean themselves and hang themselves up.'"

"She would probably say you have a really good housekeeper, and she would be right."

"Good. Ah, you are the best there ever was, is, and will be in my book, and you can take that to the bank. I don't know if I have told you this enough, and I don't think I can, but I would not even think of doing this without you. And with that I wish you a very good night and pleasant thoughts."

"Good night and pleasant dreams to you too."

With that it started to rain. I rolled over and looked at Athena, who was in the rain with no umbrella shield. She hadn't used one since that second night. I considered that she might like the rain. I wondered how long she would let it rain. And with that I fell asleep.

The next morning, I got up, used the bathroom, put on my clothes, and made my way to the kitchen. "Athena, would you turn my stove top into a griddle? I would like to make some pancakes. And I would also like to make the mix, so if you would, please, beam the ingredients to the countertop." The griddle appears along with all the ingredients. "Thank you."

I mixed up my batter and cooked up a stack of pancakes. I then went to the table and asked, "Athena, would you harvest me a small bowl of berries so I can pour them over my pancakes, and could I get a large glass of milk and a big mug of coffee?" The berries and the drinks appeared. "Thank you."

I poured the berry mix over my pancakes and started eating. I finished eating and got up from the table and walked over to Athena, and she brought up the hologram of the field.

"Athena, those berries were perfect. Man, they were good. How's everything going?"

"I have learned some things about the battle and some of the civilizations that were in it—not a lot, but some. I should be done this afternoon about thirteen hundred."

For the next several hours, I watched the hologram. A little after twelve o'clock, I decided to go the house to grill up a couple of hot dogs with all the fixin's and have some potato salad, coleslaw, and corn on the cob, along with a lager.

"Athena, that was some delicious food. Thank you. I'm glad you got me jogging. It is a good thing you can control my metabolism with those supplements you put in my food, or else I would be getting fat. I don't even notice them."

"You're welcome. I have finished the scans and compiled the data."

Athena brought up a new hologram and started her analysis. *"Instead of Medios we will call them The Conceited Ones [the Latin name was way too long: 'ones in superbiam elatus'], the civilization from the binary star system with the center planet and the forty other civilizations, came about faster-than-light travel about the same time, and they didn't like each other much. The Conceited Ones were a very aggressive race and took what they wanted from the others and started to demand everyone else to follow their rule. The missing civilization is the race I believe introduced the plant life to The Conceited Ones' world, and that's all they did; it was a preemptive strike on their part. No one knew of this civilization, and they wanted to keep it that way, so they struck first to keep their secret. While the Conceited Ones were fighting the plants to keep them from taking over their world, the others would attack them—not together, but one at a time. The Conceited Ones could fight them off one at time while fighting the plant life, but it was taking a toll. After thirty years, they started losing more fights than they won. They had to evacuate their planet and head for a remote part of space closer to the rim in thousands of ships. They must have found a system with a lot of resources to build that gigantic ship of theirs, and it took them eight hundred years to do it. When they returned, they started to attack each race's sun. In a matter of twenty or so years, they had caused all thirty-nine suns to become giant red stars and destroy all their home worlds."*

"Stand by. I think I have found the system the Conceited Ones went to, according to my new star charts. There are four red giants and a couple of dead stars surrounding a system about twenty-five hundred light years from here, and the best that gigantic ship could do is warp ten. It took it two and half years to get back. It wasn't the fastest ship; the others had somewhat faster ships."

"We might have to pay a visit to that system," I said. "Okay, continue with your analysis if you please."

"After disrupting the others' stars, they set out looking for the refugees to subjugate them so they couldn't do what they did and build up a force to come back and destroy their ship. They didn't think that the others would even think about a couple of them joining up, let alone all the races joining up, which is what they did. After a couple of years looking for them, they did come close a couple of times. The Thirty-Nine civilizations had led them on false, misleading trails. The Conceited Ones accidently found the Missing Ones and started heading for them. When word got out that the Conceited Ones were heading to the Missing Ones' system and the Missing Ones were evacuating their system, the Thirty-Nine civilizations planned their attack. It wasn't a very good plan; they were just going to come at them with all their ships—about two hundred thousand of them. When the Thirty-Nine civilizations' fleet entered the system, the Conceited Ones' ship had already drained the two suns' fuel and had destroyed three of the four planets in this system. As the fleet approached the ship, it turned and fired its primary weapon, destroying a quarter of the fleet. It took only about thirty seconds to recharge with all the fuel it had aboard. When it fired the second time, it took out another quarter of the fleet, and that's when we showed up—when they were recharging for the third time."

"What did the First Ones think we were going to do, block that shot, putting us right in front of that big stinking gun?" I asked. "Gee whiz. That was probably because that's when their outer shield was at its weakest—right there after it had just fired."

"They probably thought we would do what we did do—damage it from within. They got us inside of their main shield so we could figure out how to overload the main weapon. That Dreadnought that was chasing and shooting us—if it hadn't been chasing us, it would have been with the rest of the big dreadnoughts that attacked that ship's big secondary guns and probably would have been too badly damaged to take out the last big secondary gun, which it did after we left. With that dreadnought and the rest of the ships, it was able to take out that ship and to survive with what they had. I do

believe that none of the Conceited Ones survived the battle and that the fourth planet broke up from the crossfire."

"That dreadnought probably thought we were one of the Conceited Ones' ships coming from that gigantic ship, since we didn't look like one of the Thirty-Nine civilizations and we were headed away from that ship and inside of their main shield. (pause) Maybe that's why they were building all those drones when we showed up at their system; they probably thought we were the Conceited Ones, checking them out. Uh oh, we probably scared them into thinking that the Conceited Ones have returned. We had better get back there and let them know somehow that we helped them back then and we are not the Conceited Ones."

"Changing course and proceeding at warp forty," Athena stated. "We should be there by this time tomorrow."

"Good. Prepare a report to tell them how we got there in time, what we did, and what we learned. And is there anything we can do to reassure them that we are not the Conceited Ones?"

"I have detected scans from the Thirty-Nine civilizations' system. They are searching for something. They won't be able to detect us unless we send out a signal, and I can do that tomorrow about Oh eight hundred."

"Good, right after breakfast. Can you send that report at that time?"

"Yes, they should get it right away."

"Okay, I'm going for a run, and then I'll have supper and relax in the pond."

After supper, I didn't go to the pond. Instead Athena and I went to the computer room and reviewed the data on that gigantic ship. She put up a hologram of that ship and put it back together.

"That thing was huge," I said.

"Yes. The main section of the ship was a sphere that was twelve thousand kilometers in diameter that housed the power source. It was actually a microsun about six thousand kilometers in diameter. They fueled it using other stars. With each star, it became more powerful. In front of the sphere was a cylinder that was twelve thousand kilometers long and six thousand kilometers in diameter, with a tunnel running down the center of the cylinder that was two thousand kilometers in diameter. Also coming from the sphere were ten equally spaced cylinders about ten thousand meters in diameter, running alongside the main cylinder and stretching twenty thousand meters beyond the front of the ship. An additional four thousand meters more of the cylinders angled inward with a sixteen-thousand-meter diameter sphere at the end of each one. This may have been to augment the main beam traveling down the center of the tunnel. We never got to see it fire, but we have seen the end result. As to how they drew the elements out of the stars, I have no idea right now. I do have some data on it, but not much—just enough of the recharging sequence to cause it to overload. Then, on the opposite side of the sphere from the forward cylinder, there was another cylinder, though not as big—only four thousand kilometers long and four thousand kilometers in diameter—but it had a hundred massive engines attached to the end of it. There were dual ion cannon turrets every five hundred kilometers in between the ten smaller cylinders in front of the sphere, and about eighty dual ion cannon turrets behind the sphere on the aft cylinder with about the same spacing. All these were their secondary guns, about two hundred eighty of them, and these were big cannons. They make World War II's Big Bertha rail cannon look like a pop gun. Plus there were other turrets for close-range support for the ion cannons and other vital parts of the ship. The Thirty-Nine civilizations had just enough big Dreadnoughts left to have a turret for each ship. There would have been a lot more survivors if they had communicated better with each other. As it was, they were almost wiped out. They had the ships to take on that ship but lacked the coordination to pull it off."

After Athena's report, we went back to the house. I took a shower and went to bed.

The next morning, I got up and had a nice breakfast of a ham steaks, two eggs over easy with toast, a glass of tomato juice, and a mug of coffee. We went to the computer room and started going over things to get ready for our encounter with the Thirty-Nine civilizations.

At eight o'clock, Athena reported, *"They have detected the false signal. Sending message ... They are asking us to stop."*

"Okay, I guess we'd better stop."

Athena had already started to bring *Stingray* to a stop.

"There are three drones approaching us," Athena said. A few seconds elapsed. *"Oops, they just passed us. I will put out a transponder-like signal so they can track us better ... They are turning around. They each have established their own orbit. They are trying to scan us, but they cannot penetrate the hull. They have found my scanner access points. Should I allow them access? I can keep them out."*

"No, don't let them in yet; we should find out more about them first."

"Agreed. Until we know what their intentions are, we should keep them out."

"Let them know that we mean them no harm and that until we know them better we will not allow them access."

"They are asking for access to prove we are not a member of the Conceited Ones' civilization."

"How are we going to prove that? Anyway, we can contact the First Ones to help us out with this."

"I can try to contact the beacon to see if—Stand by. The beacon just sent a message to them, telling them who we are and what we did."

"Anything happening?"

"They have recalled their drones and have stopped making other drones. They have made over thirty million. They are now becoming part of the defense shield. That must be their standby position. They have resumed their passive scanning. That is all for now, I guess."

After an hour of waiting, I said, "Athena, how long do you think we should wait?"

"I say we should stay here for twenty-four hours and then go to this system—which is not far at about nineteen light years away—and explore it. It will take less than a day at warp twenty to get there. I will leave the transponder on so they can track us. I think waiting a month should be long enough."

"Yeah, a month should be long enough. Well, it's close enough to noon for lunch, so let's go back to the house."

After lunch, Athena and I spent a couple of hours going over some more data on the thirty-nine civilizations. The thirty days would provide plenty of time for them to contact us if they wanted. When we finished going over the data, I went for a jog and got in the pond. After relaxing in the pond for about an hour, I got out and headed to the house. By the time I got there, I was completely dry. I got dressed and sat at the table.

"Athena, I think I will have a shrimp cocktail and a steak with american fries, steamed broccoli and carrots, a tall stein of lager, and, for dessert, a cherry pie with a scoop of ice cream." The meal appeared. "Wow, that looks good. Thank you."

After supper, I walked over to Athena. "Athena, have you seen any sign of that fortieth civilization? Anything from the First Ones or even from the database of the Thirty-Nine civilizations?"

"No, there is no evidence of them in any star charts or anybody's database."

"I wonder what happened to them. I guess we have to keep an eye out for them when we resume our exploration of space. Speaking of exploration, what do you have on the ships of the thirty-nine civilizations that were in the battle?"

For the next several hours, we went over all the ships that were in the battle, including the one that chased us. Athena had been able to reconstruct the ships from the database and from the scans during our brief trip into the past.

"There was a variety of ships," Athena said. *"It was the greatest mismatch mix of ships you ever saw—a lot worse than the Nebula. There must have been over two hundred thousand ships of the Thirty-Nine civilizations that tried to engage the Conceited Ones' gigantic ship. Half of them never got to fire a shot."*

As I looked at the time and realized it was close to twenty-three hundred hours, I decided to call it a night and went back to the house to take a shower and go to bed.

CHAPTER NINETEEN

The Lost Ones

The next morning after breakfast, Athena and I went to computer room. We went over the course to that system, which she had mentioned earlier.

"It's nine o'clock," I said. "If nothing is happening, we might as well go."

"Nothing is happening. Setting course and slowly accelerating to warp twenty."

We spent the rest of the morning going over the data of the Thirty-Nine civilizations from the First Ones to see what we could learn from their contact with them. We learned they liked to be left alone. So that afternoon we spent the time in the park, fine-tuning it. I tested the fruit trees. We talked about putting in some real animals, but we talked ourselves out of it. I did seriously think about some fish, but that would have been too easy. I went to bed early that night.

For the next two weeks, we scanned the system until there was nothing left to scan. There wasn't that much to scan in the first place. At the end of the fourteenth day, we went to another system.

Athena found a system we could explore. *"It's about seventy-five light years from here, and it will take only three and half days to get there at warp twenty. I will leave the transponder on so they can still track us. But it looks interesting."*

For the other two weeks, we did the same thing to this system— we scanned everything.

"It's been four weeks and we've heard nothing from them," I said. "I guess they do want to be left alone. You said you may have the star system that the Conceited Ones fled to?"

"Yes, about twenty-four hundred light years from here. At wrap thirty we can be there in a little over thirty-two days."

"Okay, you can turn off the transponder once we leave this next system; they are not going to contact us. Let's start exploring."

"Aye, aye. Setting course and accelerating to warp thirty."

It took us a month to get to that region of space where the red stars and the dead ones were—the region we believed the Conceited Ones had fled to. Right in the middle of them was an empty sector of space big enough for a small solar system to exist. As we got closer, we notice a big black mass of something. It appeared to be liquid. The closer we got, the more solid it appeared. Once it started to change and our scanner still couldn't detect it, we stopped. We did not want to get any closer to something big and moving that the scanner couldn't detect. In fact, we started backing away from it.

"Let's keep a safe distance from it," I said.

"What would you like to consider as a safe distance?"

"Oh, about a half light year at least."

"Okay. At this range, I can no longer visually detect it."

"Really? that's strange."

"At this distance I detect nothing. As we got closer, I could visually detect it, but that was the only way I could detect it. Stand by ... Someone or something is trying to copy all my data. For the past few months, I have been developing technology to protect my database so people just can't download or upload to my database without me knowing about it and blocking any access to my source code. They are still trying. Should I let them have it?"

"Just do what you are comfortable with," I said. I then saw something out of the corner of my eye. *"What was that?"*

"They are taking too much. I can't stop them. I have detected something too. We are being boarded. How are they doing this? This is im—"

I was coming to and on the floor. I looked over to Athena, and her sphere was also on the floor, flickering.

"Athena, are you, all right?"

Athena's sphere stopped flickering, and she started to hover.

"Yes. Checking you. Good, you're okay. That was a jolt."

"Yes, it was." As I stumbled to my feet, I asked, "Can you tell where we are?"

"Stand by. We are at our Alpha station, and we appear to be intact. I have a message from the First Ones. It says, 'Sorry for the bumpy ride, but we had to get you out of there. They don't like visitors.' We were out for less than five minutes."

"They transported us that far in less than five minutes? I'd like to know how they did that."

"There is a file attached to the message," said Athena. "Oh wow, it is the formula for a jump drive. This may take a few years to figure out, but I think I can get it to work."

"Does it evolve time travel?"

"Yes."

"Time travel gives me a headache."

"By the looks of this formula, it's going to give me one too."

"Let's rest a few days and then we can start exploring again," I said. "We still have a lot of room for your diamond collection."

ABOUT THE AUTHOR

Mark J. Curtis was raised in the Midwest, the oldest son of a truck driver. After graduating from high school, Curtis joined the Air Force and served twenty years as a jet engine mechanic. Post-Air Force, he worked twelve years on heavy equipment and eventually became disabled. He retired, went back to school, and now writes.

Printed in the United States
By Bookmasters